Katie Spatz

Jenny, the Fire Maker

Jenny,

the

Fire

Maker

by Valeria Griffith

Illustrated by Jacqueline Tomes

J. B. LIPPINCOTT COMPANY
Philadelphia and New York

7336

For Jenny

CONTENTS

Jenny, the Fire Maker

1

Meet Jenny Will

WHEN the taxi delivered Jenny Will and her parents at the airport the jet was already waiting on the runway. They walked out to the gate. The jet looked enormous. With no trouble at all Jenny could imagine it to be a great, snorting, fire breathing monster, sunlight flashing off its sleek, silver sides.

She stopped and her parents stopped, too. "Are you all right, Jenny?" her mother said anxiously.

Jenny swallowed. "Oh sure. Yes. I'm just fine."

Her father put his hand on her shoulder and gave her a quick proud smile.

"I wish we could go with you," Mrs. Will said. "But of course you'll get along splendidly. You're such a brave girl. Just like your father."

The passengers were streaming out to the jet. Jenny went with them. She turned back to wave to her parents. They looked small and far away. On the outside, Jenny thought, she might seem like her father —brave, but on the inside she was more like her mother—timid. She was swept along up the steps and into the plane.

Her seat was by the window and when she looked out and down the concrete air-strip seemed surprisingly far below. And we haven't even left the ground yet, Jenny thought in some dismay.

An old gentleman had taken the seat beside her. He peered from under bristling eyebrows. "Traveling all alone, little lady?" he asked.

Jenny nodded. The plane began to move and a shiver went through Jenny right from her feet to the top of her head.

"Now don't you worry one little bit. There's not one little thing to be afraid of," the old gentleman said in a soothing voice as if he might be talking to a very small child.

"Oh, I'm not afraid," Jenny said brightly. "My goodness, this isn't my first trip on a plane. I've flown before."

"Well, then you know just what to expect."

Jenny nodded again. Actually she had been quite young when she had made that other trip by plane.

Meet Jenny Will

All she could remember was sitting close to her father and licking a sucker the stewardess had given her and thinking that all the world below looked like Grandmother Will's patchwork quilt.

The jet was gathering speed. Jenny ventured another look from the window at the concrete streaking wildly past. She closed her eyes and drew back.

"Going to take a little nap, are you?" the old gentleman said approvingly. "A good idea. I'll do the same myself."

But Jenny wasn't napping. She was thinking. It was a week ago that things began to happen that had

practically turned her world upside down. It was exactly one week ago. She remembered very well because it was the last day of school before summer vacation.

That morning she had wakened early and tiptoed through the hall, past the rattle of her father's typewriter behind the closed study doors. From the big front window in the living room she had looked down at the park eight stories below and seen that it was a fine sunny day. The fountains shot jets of water, birds swooped and the early morning park bench sitters were already assembling.

Jenny sat for a minute on the floor, her chin supported by her crossed arms on the window sill. At eye level Mike swam around in his glass bowl. Mike was her pet goldfish. Dogs and cats were not allowed in the apartment building.

She could hear her mother in the kitchen cooking breakfast for the family. She could also hear Mrs. Hinkle, the cleaning woman, singing mournfully as she scoured the bathroom. The street below was becoming crowded with taxis and trucks and buses. Their whine and rumble reached up to the window. Time to get dressed for school.

And then what had happened? Oh yes. Jenny remembered that she had gone back to her room and found that in cleaning out her room Mrs. Hinkle had cleaned out her entire nature collection as well. Jenny sped to her mother with the news but it was too late. Mrs. Hinkle had already disposed of everything in the incinerator.

When Jenny's father came to breakfast he was sympathetic and curious. "How did it happen?"

"I had my collection in the wastepaper basket," Jenny explained.

"The wastepaper basket?" Mrs. Will repeated. "What an odd place for a nature collection."

"I upset it in there last night and planned to get it out first thing this morning but I was too late."

"Too bad," Mr. Will shook his head. "What all did you lose?"

"Everything," Jenny said. "The cotton boll Mavis brought me from Texas, the buckeyes I found on the hike, the little pieces of robin's eggshell, the—"

"I doubt that our insurance covers such items," her father said. "I'm really sorry about it though, Jenny."

Mrs. Will set the first stack of pancakes on the table. "I wish you could have seen the nature collection I had when I was just eleven—your age, Jenny. It filled all the shelves on one side of my room. You see I'd already been to Camp Tanda for two summers and we'd learned about things like that. Birds and trees, rocks and stars, and the traditions of the Indians."

Jenny, wiping the dribble off the syrup pitcher sighed enviously. She glanced up and caught the look her father and mother were exchanging. It was one of those "parent" looks that meant they were planning something. Well, all one could do was be patient with them. Eventually she would find out.

"I loved every minute of those summers," Mrs. Will went on. "The overnight hikes, the council fires on Indian Rock, swimming. It was all wonderful."

Jenny laid down her fork. "I wish I could go to Camp Tanda. I wish I could spend the summer there." Jenny wished this out loud every single time her mother spoke of the exciting adventures she used to have at camp.

"But Jenny," her father said, "Camp Tanda is so far away. How would you get there?"

"On a train or perhaps a plane," Jenny said grandly. "A jet. Yes, I'd go on an enormous big jet. I'd make the trip all by myself."

"What an adventurous child you are," her mother said in wonder and admiration.

Her father said, "Jenny, your mother and I—"

Mrs. Will interrupted him. "Not until tonight, Peter. We'll talk about it then. Now Jenny has only a few minutes to get ready for school."

Jenny was both sorry and glad about it being the last day. It would be nice to have a vacation from studying but she would miss all her friends at school. None of them lived near and most of them had plans that would take them out of the city for the summer. Jenny was already lonely for them by the time she reached home in the afternoon.

Mrs. Hinkle was just leaving and met her at the door. "Your folks went out," she said. "They'll be back soon."

Jenny walked slowly through the living room and looked down at the park. Some children were playing there. But they were young ones with nurses. Jenny sighed. What would she do all summer? She opened a box of fish food and held a tiny flake at the surface of the water in the bowl. Mike came up at once and took it from her fingers. "I wish you were a girl, Mike," Jenny said, "and just my age."

She heard the apartment door open and her parents' voices. They came into the living room. "Jenny," Mrs. Will sounded excited, "we've the most wonderful surprise for you. I phoned Miss Holly at Camp Tanda today."

"Is Miss Holly still at Camp Tanda?" Jenny asked. "Why she was there when you were. It must have been ages and ages ago."

"Only eighteen," Mrs. Will said. "That isn't so long. Anyway, she said you could come to Camp Tanda for the summer just as you've always wanted to do. And you're to make the trip alone."

"I am?" Jenny said in astonishment. "Alone? Why Camp Tanda is practically in the middle of the United States."

"I know, darling, and if you weren't such a courageous girl I wouldn't think of letting you go. Although, of course, you'll be perfectly safe."

Jenny looked from her mother to her father. "It's such a surprise."

"It's this way, Jenny," Mr. Will explained. "I've gotten an assignment to do a series of articles in Austria and your mother can make the trip with me if she wishes. We thought, since you've always been so eager to get to Camp Tanda, that this was the perfect chance for you."

"Of course you don't have to go if you don't want to," Mrs. Will said, a bit anxiously.

"What would you do if I didn't?"

Her mother looked wistful for only an instant and then smiled brightly. "Why stay here with you, of course. We'd do all sorts of nice things and have a perfectly wonderful summer."

Both her father and mother were looking at Jenny. It was the first time in her life that she had had to make a big decision that would affect the whole family. And her mother didn't fool her one bit. She wanted to go to Austria very much. And her father wanted her along. "Of course I want to go to Camp Tanda," Jenny said with a little squeak in her voice. "My goodness, I can hardly wait."

Jenny and her mother shopped for camp clothes for an entire day. Mr. Will inked Jenny's name on about a million tapes and Jenny and her mother sewed them to everything. Jenny's fingers grew sore but it was exciting to see the clothing and equipment rising in piles, ready to be packed into the new suitcase.

While they sewed Mrs. Will continued to give Jenny instructions and warnings. There were so many of them that she wondered if they wouldn't be all in a muddle in her head and she wouldn't be able to sort out one from the other. "Uncle Fred will meet the plane in Chicago and put you on the train for the camp station," her mother said, the silver thimble on her finger flashing in the late afternoon sunlight. "You remember Uncle Fred, don't you, Jenny?"

Mr. Will said, "How could she remember him? She was only five years old the last time they met."

Mrs. Will looked worried. She laid down the sewing. "Jenny, you're sure, you're very sure, that you want to go off alone to camp?"

"Very sure," Jenny said and there was a funny cold feeling in her stomach. The only time she had ever been away from her parents was the week she had spent with Grandma and Grandpa Will. And, though she had told no one, she had felt like crying every single night.

The plane was to leave in the morning. Both of her parents came in to say good night and bring her surprise going-away presents. Her mother gave her a blue leather traveling case. There was a mirror in the lid and any number of little plastic bottles and boxes. There was a tiny pair of scissors, a red leather manicure case and a wooden apple that opened, with needles and thread and a thimble inside.

Jenny's father carried in a large box. First he pulled out a flashlight that not only shot a strong beam but also flashed a repeating red light. Then he took out a canteen with a shoulder strap and then a small hatchet in a sheath. Last of all he produced a jackknife with three blades, a corkscrew, a file and a folding spoon.

"Good gracious," Mrs. Will said, looking shocked, "what is she supposed to do with all that? She's not going to be hunting lions in Africa. She's going to a very well ordered, well equipped girl's camp."

"Just as well to be prepared," Mr. Will said and he and Jenny beamed at each other.

"Oh you two," Mrs. Will laughed. "You're just alike." Then her face grew sober. "Everything's happened so fast, Jenny. I'm afraid you rather got pushed into this. If, for any reason at all, you want to change your mind, it's not too late."

"I won't change my mind," Jenny said.

"I believe I may have left water running in the sink. I'd better check." Mrs. Will hurried away. Jenny and her father exchanged smiles. There was a pretty good chance that the water was not running in the sink but that Mrs. Will hadn't wanted them to see the sparkle of tears in her eyes.

Then Jenny looked sober. "I'm sure I want to go," she said slowly, "but I can't help thinking that everything was pretty nice the way it used to be. Mother and you and I together for the summer and Saturday expeditions and evening picnics. Sometimes I wish things didn't have to change—ever."

Her father took hold of her hand. "But they do, Jenny. Time moves. Things change. The world changes and we must change, too. We must grow, not only in our bodies but in our hearts and minds."

"It's rather frightening," Jenny said. "I'm not sure I'll know how to change and grow."

"There are so many to help you. Your parents and your teachers at school and church. There will be Miss Holly at the camp and the girls. And, Jenny, there's always the possibility that you may be able to help someone else."

Beside her the old gentleman gave a little snort and

Jenny opened her eyes. "Is everything all right with you?" he asked kindly.

"I think so," Jenny said.

When the plane reached Chicago Jenny got off with the other passengers and began to look rather anxiously for a tall smiling man wearing a tan straw hat with a red and purple band and a white feather. This would be Uncle Fred her mother had explained over and over.

What caught Jenny's eye was a dear little fur bear with slanting blue eyes and perky ears. It seemed to be moving toward her. She looked up. The man who carried it was tall and smiling and he wore a tan hat with—Uncle Fred!

"You must be Jenny," he said uncertainly. "You're wearing a yellow suit and a white blouse and carrying a blue traveling case just as my sister said—but you're not five years old any more!"

He saw Jenny looking at the bear and hastily thrust it behind him. "I've made a great mistake," he said. "I wanted to get you a present. Unfortunately, I've picked out one for a small child and now I find you've grown up. I do hope you'll understand. We'll get rid of it someway."

"He's a darling little fellow," Jenny said.

"And you're a charming young lady to be so polite about it," Uncle Fred said, smiling at her. "But now

22

we must get your luggage and look for a taxi. The train station is across town and we haven't too much time." He thrust the little bear into his pocket.

While the taxi sped across the city Uncle Fred pointed out places of interest. Jenny looked and listened but every once in awhile her eyes strayed to the little furry white head sticking out of Uncle Fred's pocket. Oh dear, she sighed to herself, the old gentleman on the plane thought of me as very young and now Uncle Fred thinks that I'm quite grown up. It's terribly difficult being in between.

At the station Jenny said, "What are you going to do with him, Uncle Fred?"

"Him? Who?"

"The little bear."

"Oh that." He pulled the little furry fellow from his pocket and frowned. "I really don't know. I certainly don't want to carry it around with me the rest of the day."

"I'd be glad to take him with me."

Uncle Fred's face brightened and he thrust the bear into her arms. "This is very nice of you, Jenny. Perhaps you can give it to some child on the train. Now let's see if there isn't time for a soda."

Before the train pulled in he even found time to make a dash to the newsstand and return with a big box of chocolates. "Just to show you," he said, "that

I do know the kind of present to give to a young lady."

Jenny and her possessions quite filled an entire train seat. There was her suitcase, her traveling case, books and now the bear and the box of candy. It was fortunate that the greater share of her equipment was being sent by express. She laid her jacket over the candy. The thought of it on top of the large lunch on the plane and the lemon soda made her feel slightly queer.

She rode the rest of the afternoon through green farmlands. The train seemed to sway a good deal. Jenny felt tired and a little headachy. "Maybe we'll never get there, Mr. Pong." she said to the bear. She had named him Mr. Pong because his slanting eyes gave him an oriental look. "Maybe we'll ride on forever and ever." She wondered where her father and mother were now and what they were doing.

It was late afternoon and the train almost empty when it pulled into Forest Junction. The town was very small. The station was old and about as big as a doll's house.

Miss Holly had said on the phone that there would be a counselor from the camp to meet her. Jenny looked all around for the woman but could see no one. Then across the platform she saw a green station wagon with CAMP TANDA painted on the side.

Meet Jenny Will

Getting out of the station wagon was an older girl wearing blue shorts and a white shirt just like the ones packed into her own suitcase. The girl had the most freckles and the reddest hair Jenny had ever seen.

2

Change and Challenge

JENNY was the only one getting off at Forest Junction and she was conscious of the other passengers looking out the window at her as she stood on the station platform with her bags and her bear and her big box of chocolates.

Down the platform they were unloading the rest of her things that had been checked through. It made a sizable pile and the red-headed counselor whistled as she looked at it. "Whew! It looks as if you brought everything but the kitchen sink. You must be planning a long stay at camp."

"All the rest of the summer," Jenny told her.

"I know," the girl said and then as an afterthought she added, "I'm Miss Bugs."

"How do you do Miss—Bugs," Jenny said.

"I'm called that because my major in college is entomology. Get it?"

"No."

"I study bugs."

"Oh."

Miss Bugs was loading the bags and bundles into the station wagon and Jenny had a chance for a good look at her. Somehow she hadn't expected a camp counselor to be quite like this.

Miss Bugs had packed everything in back except the box of chocolates. "I'm afraid you can't keep this," she said, putting it between them on the front seat. "We'll turn it in at the camp office."

Jenny said, "My Uncle Fred bought it for me in Chicago."

"Sorry," Miss Bugs said. "Camp rule. No extra food packages from home."

"Are there many rules at camp?"

"Quite a few, Jenny. Some of them may not seem very reasonable to you at first but they're all important. It takes rules to make the camp run properly you know. If all one hundred and fifty of the campers and staff did just what they wanted to when they wanted to, we wouldn't get anything done and we wouldn't have any fun. In fact everything would be in a terrible mess."

Miss Bugs sounded so earnest about the rules that Jenny decided not to say anything more about the candy. Though it did seem rather hard to have all of Uncle Fred's chocolates eaten up by the people in the camp office.

Miss Bugs swung the car expertly out into the street. Very soon they were traveling a narrow, winding graveled road. Dust hung over it and coated the leaves of the trees and bushes that grew thickly along the sides. It almost seemed that they were traveling through a jungle.

Miss Bugs grinned at her. "Not much like home, I bet?"

Jenny, thinking of the broad thoroughfare outside the apartment window and the heavy traffic and the big park with its fountains and neatly clipped grass, shook her head. It all seemed a million miles away.

"I know you've never been to Camp Tanda before, Jenny, but have you ever been to any camp?"

Jenny shook her head. "I've always wanted to though," she said firmly. "I like faraway places and strange adventures. My goodness, I'd like to go to Africa and hunt lions if I had the chance."

Miss Bugs looked at her with some surprise. "Well, good for you," she said.

There was a rustle in the weeds and a strange animal moved out onto the roadway. Jenny yelped and clutched Miss Bugs. Miss Bugs shouted with laughter. "No, it isn't a lion," she said. "Only a groundhog."

Jenny was pink with embarrassment and said nothing.

Miss Bugs looked down at Mr. Pong, partially concealed by Jenny's jacket. "Awfully cute bear. The girls in Seven Stripe cabin will be crazy about him. Almost every one of them has some kind of a stuffed animal on her bed."

Jenny brought Mr. Pong into plainer view. She glanced up at Miss Bugs. "I suppose they'll laugh about my being scared by that groundhog."

Miss Bugs said, "If I were you I wouldn't tell them."

Jenny had a feeling that she was going to like Miss Bugs very, very much. After a minute she said, "I thought the girls slept in tents."

"Some of the older groups do. The ones doing primitive camping, but your group, the Shady Glade girls, are in cabins."

"My mother slept in a tent when she was here," Jenny said. "She told me that everyone did then. And they all went boating and swimming together in the river and at night they cooked their meals over campfires and then they sat around them and sang."

Miss Bugs looked at Jenny, "That must have been a long time ago."

"Ages and ages," Jenny agreed.

"The camp has changed quite a bit." They had reached the top of a steep hill and Miss Bugs drove the car to one side of the road. "You can see the whole layout from here."

Jenny looked and wondered if Miss Bugs was trying to fool her. Was that really Camp Tanda? Her mother had told her of a dear little camp nestled on a wooded hillside close by the water. What Jenny saw now was a vast expanse of grounds and buildings. "The swimming pool is over there," Miss Bugs said, pointing. "And there are the kitchens and the dining hall and that way is the health lodge and next the administration building. The big round building with the totem pole is our new assembly hall. That meadow in the woods is where we have our council fires. The lodges and sleeping quarters of the different units are mostly hidden by the trees. The girls who live in teepees are over that way and be careful not to wander into their Indian Village for if you do they'll put paint on your face. The Shady Glade girls and the little papooses in Happy Valley all live beyond the swinging bridge."

"Oh my," Jenny said. She had that strange empty feeling again. "I didn't know Camp Tanda was so big."

As they watched, doors on every side of the dining hall opened and double lines of girls streamed out and hurried in different directions. "It's later than I thought," Miss Bugs said. "Tonight is Council Fire and everyone will be in a great hurry to get ready. We'd better get clicking ourselves." She headed the car down the hill.

"I'd like to take you over to the cabin first so that you could meet some of the girls," Miss Bugs said, "but we'd better rush to the dining hall if we want anything to eat."

The vast room was empty except for the cooks

working behind the counter. One of them handed out two plates of beef, mashed potatoes, sweet corn, salad and filled two glasses with milk. Carrying hers, Jenny followed Miss Bugs to a table at the side of the room. "Do all of the girls eat here?" she asked, looking at the lines of tables each bearing a long pole with a number.

"Everyone," Miss Bugs told her, "from the smallest papoose to the largest counselor. We all get to know each other that way and that's the way Miss Holly likes it." She looked at her own empty plate and then at Jenny's untouched one. "You haven't eaten a thing."

"I can't. I'm not hungry," Jenny said rather anxiously and hoped that Miss Bugs would not insist on her eating everything the way they did at school. She didn't really feel sick but it wouldn't take much to make her that way.

To her relief Miss Bugs said, "Okay. Then mind if I have it?" She switched their plates and in a short time one was as bare as the other. "Camp life builds up your appetite," Miss Bugs said and Jenny, watching her spread peanut butter on the last slice of bread, thought that it certainly must be true.

"Miss Holly wanted to see you just as soon as you arrived," Miss Bugs said. "Your mother was quite a favorite of hers, you know."

Jenny smiled. "My mother has told me a lot about Miss Holly."

Miss Bugs looked at her watch. "I guess it's too late to go to her cabin now. She'll be on her way to the Council Fire and so should we. Come on. Maybe some of the girls will still be at Seven Stripe cabin, though I doubt it. Everyone's heading for the meadow."

The cabin was empty when they got there. It was more like a screened porch than anything else. Except for the screening it was open on all four sides with canvas curtains rolled to the roof. Two rows of beds faced each other across a narrow aisle and each of them was a welter of socks and ties and shorts and assorted gear.

"Too bad you had to see the cabin first like this," Miss Bugs said cheerfully. "It's because I wasn't here to prod the girls into putting their stuff away. But you should see it at inspection time. Not a thing out of place and the blankets so tight you could bounce an egg on them. That's why this is called Seven Stripe cabin. One year we won inspection seven weeks in a row.

"That's my little den behind the partition and you're to have the bed in the corner. The washroom is down the hill. It's got a sign on it, 'The Crystal Palace.' That's because it's got a plastic roof. Take your towel with you. You'll find a place for it on the line outside the door."

Jenny, confused and practically breathless from trying to remember everything, located her towel and soap and started down the steep path outside the door. There were woods in every direction as far as she could see. She looked behind her. The cabin she had just left was already out of sight. "Oh my," she said, "it's not at all the way I thought it would be."

said. "That's the quickest way."

The long bridge was suspended over a deep ravine. It creaked and swayed when they crossed and the boards seemed to rise under Jenny's feet like the swell of the ocean. If the meadow seemed dusky, the ravine was a dark chasm. Jenny shivered a little and was glad when they reached the end.

They came out on a small rise. Jenny could see a circle outlined by stones. At the center of the circle was the tower of logs she had seen from the hillside.

"That's the council ring, Jenny. We're too late to join our group now. Stand here a minute and watch." Miss Bugs whispered although they were far from anyone. A bird chirped in the bushes and somewhere nearby in the grass there was a rustle like a small animal moving warily. Jenny stood closer to Miss Bugs.

The twilight was fast slipping away. At a distance from the council ring Jenny could make out a blurred rim of white almost hidden by the thick surrounding trees. It was the shirts of the campers who sat in a great circle three deep and quietly waited.

From within the ring came a long sweet call, rising and falling, and finally trailing away into the silence. From the woods came an answering call and then two flames appeared. As they grew closer and brighter Jenny could see that they were torches carried by girls dressed as Indians. Behind them came a drummer controlling the pace of the procession with a strong echoing beat. Other girls in Indian costume followed. Around their ankles were bands of bells so that as they stepped to the beat of the drum the air was filled with a steady rhythmical chiming. As the group approached the council ring Jenny shivered with excitement and Miss Bugs put her hand on her shoulder. "Let's go on now," she whispered again.

They made their way to the outer circle of girls. One of them, older than Jenny, slid over so that she could share the poncho that covered the dew-soaked grass.

The procession came to the center of the ring and the torch bearers thrust their fire into the tower of wood. It caught with a hiss and a roar and flames shot skyward. The council ring became a circle of light. What Jenny had supposed to be a tree at the edge of the circle was in fact a great brightly lighted totem pole.

The drumming faded away and a woman, dressed in the long brown robe of the Indians, came forward so that Jenny could see her plainly. "Miss Holly," Jenny whispered. Miss Holly was exactly as her mother had described her.

It was a long ceremony with dances and singing. Girls went forward to receive their honors and then came back to their places whispering happily to close neighbors. No one spoke to Jenny. She was very tired. She now saw the council ring and the flames of the fire in a kind of blur. Overhead the stars had come out and made a diamond-studded canopy above the meadow.

Then it was all over and the girls began to move away from the circle of stones. Jenny couldn't see Miss Bugs so she followed a group back toward the swinging bridge.

At the first sound of a bugle every girl stopped and stood motionless as the clear solemn notes swept over the meadow. The last note fell away into a silence so complete that Jenny could hear the croaking of frogs in a nearby pond and the faraway barking of a dog. Then from a hilltop a bugle answered and from another hill the call was repeated.

It was like the breaking of a spell. At once the girls began to gather in little chattering groups and move off arm in arm.

Jenny stood at the end of the bridge and watched anxiously for Miss Bugs.

4

☼

Mosquito Trouble

WHEN Miss Bugs met up with Jenny at the swinging bridge she was accompanied by all the girls of Seven Stripe cabin. "This is Carol," she said, "and Sally and June and Mary and Nadine and–oh, bother, what's the use? You can't see them in the dark anyway, Jenny."

"You'll just have to sort us out later, Jenny," one of the girls said. Jenny tried hard to see her face. She had such a nice friendly voice.

Back at the cabin Miss Bugs rushed them into bed-time preparations. "Thirty minutes until lights out, kids. And I don't want you to be late again. One more demerit and we won't get to go on that cook-out tomorrow. Jenny, better get your bed made up."

The cot was quite narrow and Jenny's sheets much too wide. She tried hard to turn the corners under neatly but she saw that she was doing a very bad job of it and she felt that all of the girls must be watching her. She felt terribly embarrassed and shy and scarcely looked at them but kept her head bent over the bed.

"Want some help, Jenny?"

"No, thanks," she said briskly. "I can manage all right by myself."

In the momentary silence she heard one of the girls say, "If she doesn't manage any better than that we'll never win cabin inspection so long as she's here."

"Oh, be still, Nadine," someone else whispered.

Jenny's face grew hot. She opened her suitcase and pretended very hard to be looking for something. She ignored the girls completely.

Miss Bugs said, "Okay, gals, off to bed. That's the last word on it and I mean it."

There was considerable giggling but at last the girls were settled in bed and Miss Bugs retired behind her partition. From her cot Jenny could look out and see other lighted cabins like Seven Stripe. Simultaneously lights went out and taps sounded across the valley.

Jenny lay stiff and quiet on her bed and one by one the girls around her stopped whispering and fell asleep. They were all friends, Jenny thought. They had each other and she didn't have anyone. They didn't even want her in the cabin. A terrible ache rose up inside her that was worse than a stomach-ache and a headache and an earache all at the same time.

Her mother hadn't known it would be like this or she wouldn't have sent her. She wondered where her father and mother were now. It was Tuesday night. In a few short hours they would be getting on the great jet that would take them far, far away across the ocean.

Jenny felt the sob rising in her throat but not until it was too late to turn her head and bury it in the pillow. She waited anxiously to see if anyone had heard her. The girls' breathing was as regular as before but from behind the partition came Miss Bugs' voice. "Jenny?"

"Yes," Jenny said, swallowing.

There was a pause. "Jenny," Miss Bugs said again, "did you hear that mosquito?"

"Mosquito?" Jenny repeated, surprised. "No, I didn't hear any mosquito."

"Well, I did," Miss Bugs came around the partition. "If there's anything I can't stand in the middle of the night it's a mosquito. It drives me mad, mad, mad!"

The girl on the cot next to Jenny's, rolled over and pulled herself up on one elbow. "What is it?" she said sleepily. "Is it morning?"

"It's a mosquito, Carol," Miss Bugs said in a hoarse

whisper. "And it's driving me mad, mad, mad!"

Jenny sat up, too. In the moonlight she could see Miss Bugs plainly. She wore short pajama pants and a kind of long shirt over them. She ran both hands through her hair so that it bushed up all over.

"Hold the flashlight, Jenny," Miss Bugs ordered. "Flash it over there. I'll see if I can get him." Jenny flashed the light and Miss Bugs, dashing down the aisle ended up against the partition with a great thump. Now all the girls were awake and scrambling from their beds.

Mosquito Trouble

"What is it? What's happening?"

"Miss Bugs and Jenny are chasing a mosquito," Carol told them.

Jenny shot the light here and there while Miss Bugs, in a perfect fury, charged up and down the aisle, thwacking and swatting while the girls shrieked and got out of her way. Finally she braced herself for a mighty leap and then landed right in the middle of Carol's cot. With a crash Miss Bugs and the cot hit the floor. Slowly she sat up, shook her hair out of her eyes and let out a sigh. "I got it," she said happily.

With Miss Bugs on the floor and the bed in pieces it seemed terrible to be laughing but Jenny couldn't help it. She laughed until the tears came into her eyes. Luckily the other girls were laughing, too, and Miss Bugs didn't seem to mind. She got up and tried to put the bed together but as soon as she got one end together the other fell apart.

"It's hopeless," she said at last. "We'll have to find another bed for Carol or stand her in the corner for the night. Let's see, maybe the best thing is for me to sleep in Jenny's bed and then Jenny and Carol can sleep together in mine because it's bigger."

With much commotion the change was made. Jenny and Carol climbed into the counselor's bed and then Sally came around the partition carrying Mr. Pong. She handed the white bear to Jenny. "I rescued this fellow from your cot," she explained. "If Miss Bugs had slept on him he would have been as smashed as that mosquito."

"Oh, thank you," Jenny said.

Sally lingered. "It's going to be lots of fun having you in our cabin. Do you want to be my partner when we go on the cook-out tomorrow?"

Carol sat up. "Jenny is going to be my partner," she announced.

Now all the girls except Nadine crowded around the corner. "That isn't fair. We'll have to draw straws to see who gets Jenny for a partner."

Miss Bugs called out, "One more peep out of any of you and I'm going to draw a buggy whip. Now get to your beds." The girls scampered.

When they were settled Carol whispered to Jenny, "Don't worry about anything that old Nadine says. She's always trying to make trouble. She comes from my town. She and June both do. It's Miss Holly's town, too. Star Center."

"Star Center is where my mother lived when she was a girl," Jenny whispered back.

"I expect Miss Holly thought of that when she assigned you to Seven Stripe cabin with June and me."

Yawning sleepily, Jenny asked, "Is a cook-out fun?"

"The very most."

5

✻

Cook-out Complications

In the middle of a very fine dream Jenny was awakened by Carol, leaning over her and shaking her shoulder. "Are you awake, Jenny? It's time to get up."

"It couldn't possibly be," Jenny said and ducked down under the covers.

"Jenny won't wake up, Miss Bugs."

"She doesn't have to." Miss Bugs' voice sounded quite close. "She had a long trip yesterday and the camp is new to her. Miss Holly said she could sleep late and that she didn't have to go on the cook-out unless she wanted to."

"But I do want to," Jenny said, throwing back the covers and sitting up so suddenly that Carol nearly fell off the bed. "I want to go and I don't mind getting up early. My goodness, I wouldn't mind getting up if it was only six o'clock in the morning."

"That's exactly what it is," Miss Bugs said. "Now speed up, girls. Put on good sturdy clothes, jeans and jackets and don't forget your ditty bags and packs and eating utensils and canteens."

"Oh gosh," Jenny said, buttoning her shirt with one hand while she fumbled through her bags with the other. She was sliding her feet into the slippers she had worn the day before when Miss Bugs came down the aisle on an inspection trip.

"You'll want to wear socks, Jenny. Otherwise you might get a blister and you'll certainly want heavier shoes than those."

"Tennis shoes?" Jenny suggested hopefully.

"Is that the heaviest you have?"

Jenny sighed. On their shopping expedition her mother had insisted on buying her some horrible looking oxfords with heavy lacings and blunt toes and flat rubber heels. Jenny had privately thought it an outrageous whim on the part of her mother and had buried the shoes at the very bottom of her suitcase where she intended them to remain until she returned home. Reluctantly she fished them out.

As she laced up the stubby oxfords she glanced secretly at the feet of the other girls and was relieved to find that some of them wore shoes as awful as hers.

Cook-out Complications

The rest of the camp was still asleep and they quietly marched single file down to the dining hall where the cooks were already beating up muffin and pancake batter. After the girls had had breakfast they collected their supplies for the cook-out lunch, rolled their packs and distributed the gear and utensils to be carried. Jenny followed the example of the other girls and slung her pack over her back and then tied her ditty bag, canteen, mess kit and frying pan to her belt.

Everything in order, they started up the winding trail behind the camp. Miss Bugs led the way with Mary, then came Sally and June, then Carol and Jenny and last of all, Nadine.

"Don't take it too fast, girls," Miss Bugs warned. "Remember the trail is steep and this is the first time Jenny has made the climb."

"Oh, it won't bother me any," Jenny said. "At home I'm a member of the Explorers' Club. My goodness, I could probably run up this trail."

"I'll just bet," Nadine muttered from behind her.

The sun was full up but not yet strong enough to steal away the dew from the bushes that bordered the trail. Hot from the climb, Jenny let the cool wet branches brush against her face and arms. Several times Miss Bugs stopped them to observe a flower growing close by or to listen to a bird call. "Who knows that one?"

"Cardinal," Mary and June said together.

Later Miss Bugs held up her hand for another halt. "And that one?"

The call was from a distance. "Drink your tea-a-a-a. Drink your tea-a-a-a."

"I think it's a ground robin," June said.

"I couldn't even hear it," Nadine said. "Back here it sounds just like walking behind a garbage truck."

Jenny stopped still. It was all too true. The other girls had quite deftly hung their gear about themselves but the things tied to Jenny's belt had all jumbled together and now with every step the canteen banged on the frying pan and the knife in her ditty bag whacked the tin utensils in the mess kit. She had hoped that no one except herself was aware of the clatter. She made an effort to put things back in their proper places but it was rather hopeless.

"Never mind," Carol said. "We're almost there."

At the top of the mountain they made camp. Miss Bugs called it a hill. She said, "We'll build our fire on Tomkins's hill." But Jenny knew perfectly well that she had just finished climbing a mountain. Gratefully she removed the noisy pans and her pack and lying flat on her stomach at the edge of the fast running stream she splashed water over her face and hands.

The other girls busily made preparations for the meal. Carol showed Jenny how to sling the food sacks over high branches to keep them out of the way of insects and animals. Mary and Sally searched for wood. Nadine, who owned a folding shovel, dug a shallow trench for a fire and Miss Bugs passed judgment on the rocks brought for her inspection. She shook her head at Jenny's. "Limestone," she said. "It might explode." Jenny dropped it hastily. "I mean in the fire. We're going to cook our eggs on them."

"But I brought a frying pan."

"That's for mixing the biscuit dough," Carol said. "Cooking on a hot rock is part of a test, Jenny. We're all working for the Camp Craft badge. It's the most important one that's awarded."

"Then I'll cook my egg on a rock, too. I want to work for the Camp Craft badge."

The girls placed the rocks and small twigs in the bottom of the hole and criss-crossed larger sticks over the top. Satisfied with their work they stepped back. Miss Bugs said, "Jenny, you may light the fire."

Everyone looked at her. This was plainly considered to be an honor. Helplessly Jenny looked back at them.

"Go on, light it, Jenny," June urged.

"I can't," Jenny's voice was a small embarrassed croak. "I've never done it. I don't know how."

The girls looked amazed. Even Miss Bugs seemed startled. "You've never lighted a fire? You mean you really don't know how? I don't understand."

"Well, I know you rub two sticks together or something like that but—"

The girls broke into shouts of laughter. "Oh, Jenny," Miss Bugs was unable to keep back a shout of her own, "I meant for you to light it with a match." She took the little tin matchbox from the pile of equipment and handed it over. The girls were still laughing. Nadine in particular was practically overcome with mirth. "Okay, kids," Miss Bugs said. "That's enough. The time may come when you'd be pretty glad to know how to start a fire with two sticks."

The fire caught, the heavy sticks were soon blazing away and the coals dropped into the trench. They kept testing the stones to determine their heat and when water splashed over them, danced on their surfaces, Miss Bugs said they were just right. The girls shoved the stones out of the trench.

Jenny pushed a piece of bacon over her rock to grease it as she saw the others do and then she watched them take the centers out of slices of bread. "We'll put the bread on the stone, drop the egg in the middle, and then we'll have toast along with our fried egg." Miss Bugs demonstrated neatly. Her egg stood up smartly in its little nest.

"I don't think I care for any toast with my egg," Jenny said and before anyone could stop her she had cracked her egg and dropped it on the rock. Instantly it spread in all directions, even running down over the sides.

"The only way you'll be able to eat that egg," Mary said, "is to eat the rock along with it."

"I'll tell you what, Jenny." Miss Bugs spoke in a very bright gay voice. "Since this is your first day in camp why don't you be our guest and let us do the cooking for you?"

The girls spiralled their biscuit dough on green sticks and held it over the bed of coals to bake. Jenny thought the biscuits delicious although they weren't quite done in the middle. Miss Bugs did let her help make the banana boats for dessert. They peeled back narrow strips of skin, slit the bananas, stuck in marshmallows and brown sugar, put the skins back in place, wrapped the whole business with aluminum foil and put them in the coals. When they unwrapped the bananas a few minutes later they were wonderfully soft and sweet and sticky.

Sally sighed with pleasure. "I wish my mother cooked things like this at home."

After lunch they cleaned up the camp area, smothered the fire and replaced the dirt and sod in the hole. "Now an hour's rest before we go on our nature hunt," Miss Bugs said. "To rest your feet why don't you take off your shoes and go wading in the creek?"

Jenny sat down and began to untie the thick laces of her oxfords. "My feet can sure use a rest. That was a terrific climb up the mountain."

"Up Tomkins's hill," Miss Bugs corrected. "But just think how much worse your feet might be feeling if I hadn't had you wear the proper shoes and socks." Whistling she went over to check the equipment pile.

Jenny slipped off her white socks. There on her right heel was a quite large and quite pink blister. She started to call to Miss Bugs and changed her mind. This was the sort of thing that so often happened to grown-ups when they were trying to do their best. Just the way her father, showing her the safe way to use a jackknife, cut his finger.

Jenny gazed thoughtfully at the blister. It simply had no business being there.

6

☼

Green Vines and Green Peas

BECAUSE of all the joking and giggling and pushing each other into the stream, the rest hour turned out to be not as restful as Miss Bugs had had in mind. At the end of forty minutes she had the girls team up to go in search of nature material for their notebooks. Nadine drew Jenny's name and made a wry face. "Just my luck to have to go with someone who doesn't know anything about nature."

"I do know something about it," Jenny said. "It was one of the chief interests of the Explorers' Club. My goodness, I even built up a nature collection of my own."

"Fine," Miss Bugs said. "What do you have in your nature collection?"

"Unfortunately," Jenny said, "it was accidentally destroyed—by fire."

"All right, girls, off we go. Sally and Mary search just below here. Carol and June go to the right and Nadine and Jenny follow the stream. I'll stay here with the gear." Miss Bugs settled herself comfortably on a log. "Remember the rules. Be particularly careful not to cross the camp boundary, stay in sight of your partner at all times and start back the minute you hear the whistle."

Nadine started along the creek and Jenny marched behind her. Almost at once the ground began to slope upward and pretty soon they were once more climbing a steep trail. "I thought we were already at the top of this mountain," Jenny said. "How many tops does it have?"

"You're not tired already, are you?" Nadine called back and quickened her pace.

"Of course not," Jenny said with a gasp and a puff. In spite of her best efforts the space between Nadine and herself continued to widen. Presently at a point where the path and stream came together she stretched out full length on the ground. She saw Nadine glance over her shoulder, hesitate and then come hurrying back. Jenny raised her head.

"Oh," Nadine said, "I thought you had fainted or something."

"I just stopped to take a drink." Jenny bent her head and scooped up water in her hands.

"You can't drink that," Nadine said sharply. "It might be polluted and besides you'd be breaking a camp rule. I'm sure I don't know what Miss Bugs would have to say about that. Drink out of your canteen."

Jenny sat up. "I left it with the gear. It seemed silly to bring along water when there's so much of it around." She looked critically at the stream splashing clear and bright over the rocks. "It looks perfectly clean to me."

"It may be," Nadine said rather smugly, "but you can't drink it." She swung her own canteen into plainer view.

Jenny looked at it. "In that case I shall have to drink some of yours."

Nadine put both hands firmly around the canteen. "Oh no, you can't do that, either. Every camper has to be responsible for her own water. That's one of the rules of survival. You couldn't expect one person to bring along water and then have others drink it up and then have that person die of thirst."

"I wouldn't be a bit surprised," Jenny said, "if I am dying of thirst this very minute. And if you don't give me a drink I shall have to break the camp rule and drink the stream even if it is—"

"Polluted."

"Yes, even if it's what you said. And if I get terribly sick or something I'm sure I don't know what Miss Bugs will have to say about that."

"Well, just a small one then." Nadine unscrewed the top and held out the canteen, keeping the strap firmly over her shoulder. Jenny managed three fast, large-sized gulps before Nadine jerked the canteen away. "We may as well get going again," she said.

"I don't believe I'm going any farther." Jenny looked around. "There must be plenty of nature material right around here. What are we supposed to be looking for?"

Nadine was still shaking the canteen and peering crossly into the small opening. "Leaves and things." She began to dart about, systematically plucking leaves from all the nearby trees and bushes. Jenny got up and did the same. She worked as hard as she could. She was determined to have just as big a pile as Nadine. After a few minutes they came back beside the stream and spread out their collections.

Nadine looked at Jenny's. "Honestly!" she said in disgust. "You're supposed to be getting different leaves. More than half of yours are scrub oak."

Jenny looked critically at the leaves in front of her. In her haste to get a lot she had not paid much attention to what it was she was gathering. Most of the

leaves did, in fact, look exactly alike.

Nadine was arranging hers into a neat pile. "Are you at Camp Tanda for just the first session or are you going to stay all summer?"

"All summer. My parents are in Austria. My father is getting material for an article. He's a writer."

"What's your mother? Just a housewife?" Before Jenny could answer Nadine said," My mother is a singer. In New York."

"Opera?" Jenny asked. "Does she sing at the Metropolitan? I went there once."

"Just because I tell you something," Nadine said, "you have to start getting nosey and asking a lot of questions. Look, there's a plant over there I bet you haven't got."

"There?" Jenny reached out and grasped it. She let go with a yelp. Her hand seemed to be full of needles.

Nadine leaned forward, her arms wrapped around her knees. "Silly. You took the wrong one. You took the stinging nettle."

"I took the one you told me to."

Nadine jumped up. "Well, I'm not just going to sit here. I'm going up the path and get one of those ash leaves."

Jenny wrapped her smarting hand in her handkerchief and watched her go. "I'm not going to like her, that's for sure."

She rearranged her leaves once more, discarding the ones which were identical. It left only a small pile. Then she saw a vine growing just beyond the path. It had glossy green pointed leaves, three to a stem. Jenny pulled a length of the vine and added it to her collection. Studying Nadine's she saw that the other girl hadn't a bit of the lovely vine. "Serves her right, too," Jenny thought. "It would serve her right if I threw all her leaves in the brook and let them float downstream." But Jenny knew this wasn't true and it gave her a kind of mean feeling even to be thinking of such a thing. It also reminded her of something her mother had told her.

Her mother had said, "Disliking a person gives me such an unpleasant feeling that I try to do something about it. I find one of the best things is to do something nice for the person without them knowing about it. It always makes me feel much better."

"I could try it," Jenny decided. Carefully she broke her vine with the glossy leaves in half and tucked Nadine's piece among the other leaves so that she wouldn't see it right away. Then Jenny sat back to see if she felt better about Nadine. She didn't very much.

It was surprisingly dark considering that it was about the middle of the afternoon. Jenny heard a clear sharp whistle, repeated three times, and then Nadine hurried down the path. She scooped up her leaves. "Come on," she said. "We're supposed to start right back when we hear that and besides it's going to rain."

The others were already at the camp site when they arrived. They loaded the gear and started down trail as fast as Miss Bugs would permit. "No running," she warned. "Someone might fall and be hurt and then we really will be delayed." In spite of their haste the rain overtook them and they had to take shelter behind some overhanging rocks. With all the thunder and lightning it was rather fun.

Just as soon as it cleared a little, Miss Bugs hurried them on. "I'm afraid we'll miss dinner," she said in such an anxious voice that they all stepped along as fast as they could just to oblige her.

The first bugle had sounded when they reached main camp and cleaning for dinner was done in a rather sketchy way. Hastily they stuffed their leaves and other nature findings into brown paper bags and carried them down to the cool nature room on their way to the dining hall.

Jenny found out that she was to be seated at Miss Holly's table. She wished that she had done a thorough job of washing instead of merely changing her shirt. But it was too late.

Just as Miss Bugs had told her there was an assortment of girls at the table. Two small ones who must be from Happy Valley, four about her own age and two girls who were quite grown up and who must be from Indian Village. Jenny hadn't met any of them.

Miss Holly sat at the end of the table, behind the platters of food. She smiled at Jenny and Jenny returned a small quick smile. It was funny. One of the things she had looked forward to most in coming to Camp Tanda was getting to know Miss Holly and now she felt rather nervous about it. She hoped Miss Holly wasn't going to talk to her a great deal and ask her questions. Not with all the girls, particularly the big ones, looking on. To her relief Miss Holly only introduced her to the others and began serving the food.

Each of them handed up her plate. Jenny sent up hers along with the rest. The roast beef looked wonderful and so did the mashed potatoes. "But no green peas, please, Miss Holly," Jenny said. "I never eat green peas." It was true that she never did. Often she had heard her mother say to people, "Jenny never eats green peas. Even when she was a little baby she pushed them right out of her mouth."

Jenny was aware of a small silence around the table. Miss Holly, with Jenny's plate in her hand, was looking at her questioningly.

One of the very small girls said, "Jenny isn't going to eat any green peas."

Miss Holly said pleasantly, "One of the things we do at Camp Tanda is eat something of everything that's served. Even if it is only a little bit."

"All right," Jenny said with a swallow. "Just a very little, please."

The plate was passed back to her. Beside the large slice of roast beef and the big pile of potatoes was one single, lonely, middle-sized green pea.

Jenny looked up into Miss Holly's bright sparkling eyes and then she and everyone else around the table broke into laughter. Finally they quieted down.

"I'm so glad you're here, Jenny," Miss Holly said. "We're going to have such a lot of fun."

Jenny ate the pea first of all. It was absolutely delicious.

7

Nature Trouble

SEVERAL times during the night Jenny half awakened. Her arms itched. The place must be full of mosquitos although she couldn't hear any and Miss Bugs didn't seem to be troubled.

It was daylight long before the first bugle sounded. From the next cot Carol whispered, "What's the matter with you, Jenny? You keep thrashing around."

"Mosquitos, I guess. I itch. Sorry I woke you up."

"It's okay." Carol yawned. "It's too nice to be sleeping anyway."

Across the aisle Nadine grumbled, "Why don't you kids keep still?" And then it seemed that all the girls were awake.

"I guess it's my fault," Jenny said, pushing back the

covers and sitting up. "I itch terribly."

"Jenny," June squealed, "what's happened to you? What's happened to your arms?"

Jenny looked down. On each arm were several large, pink, blistery patches. "Mosquitos?" she asked hopefully.

Carol came over to Jenny's cot to examine the spots. "I never saw mosquito bites like that before."

"Maybe you've got something, Jenny," June said. "Maybe some disease."

Nadine raised her head and looked at them over the covers. Her eyes were bright and snappy. "Maybe," she said slowly and impressively, "maybe Jenny's got leprosy."

"Leprosy!" the girls repeated in whispered horror. They all looked at Jenny and she looked back at them trying to appear as brave as possible.

"You all better keep away from her so you won't catch it," Nadine advised.

The girls drew back, all except Carol who, with a defiant glance at Nadine, continued to sit on the edge of the cot. However, she leaned as far away from Jenny as it was possible to do without actually moving.

"What is leprosy?" Jenny asked in a quavering voice.

No one knew. They all looked at Nadine. "Well,"

she said, slowly raising herself to a sitting position, "I don't know exactly what leprosy is but I do know it's perfectly dreadful."

Carol said suddenly, "If Jenny's got it then so have you, Nadine." Sure enough on the back of one of Nadine's hands was a high blistery patch. A similar one was on her other wrist.

Nadine said, "Oh, no!"

Just then Miss Bugs came around the corner of the partition. Her eyes were only half open and she was so sleepy she didn't walk quite straight. "Whatever is going on in here? It's another thirty minutes until first bugle."

"I'm sorry to have to tell you, Miss Bugs," Jenny said, "but I'm afraid Nadine and I have the leprosy."

Miss Bugs' eyes flew open. She looked even more stunned than the girls. Jenny began to wonder if there was any hope at all.

Miss Bugs shooed Carol away and sat down beside Jenny. She looked carefully at the spots. "Honey, I'm pretty sure it's poison ivy." She looked Nadine over. "Don't scratch it and we'll send you down to the Health lodge and have Miss Molly, the nurse, look at it."

Now that Jenny knew she couldn't scratch them, the spots itched even more than before. Miss Bugs said, "I don't see how you ever got into it. We thought the camp was completely clear of the stuff. It must have been when you two went upstream yesterday. Nadine, you certainly know poison ivy."

"Of course I do," Nadine said. "I learned that my first week here. I wouldn't go near it."

An awful thought came to Jenny. "Is poison ivy a green viney stuff?"

"Yes," Miss Bugs said.

"With shiny pointed leaves?"

"Three to a stem," Miss Bugs added.

The truth must be revealed. "I picked some for my nature collection," Jenny said. The girls groaned.

"Well, I wasn't silly enough to pick any for my collection," Nadine said excitedly. "How did it get on me?"

Jenny took a deep breath. This was going to be the worst of all. "I wanted to give you a nice surprise, Nadine, so while you were up the path getting an ash leaf I divided my poison ivy and put half in your pile."

Nadine looked as if she was going to explode. "A nice surprise! Oh boy! Oh, sure!"

Later the nurse pronounced Miss Bugs' diagnosis to be correct. The girls did indeed have poison ivy. Miss Molly treated Nadine first and sent her to wait in the office and then she took care of Jenny. She looked her over quite carefully to be sure she hadn't missed anything and saw the pink spot on her heel.

"Oh, dear," she said, "you've also gone and gotten a blister. How can we ever convince you girls to wear proper footgear on your trail hikes?"

Jenny considered telling her the whole story, starting back at home when her mother carefully shopped for the frightful oxfords. But it was a long story and not worth the trouble. Besides it would keep Nadine waiting even longer for her breakfast and she was cross enough already. As she had every right to be.

Miss Molly walked to the dining hall with them. "Remember what I told you to do. Come and see me this afternoon, don't get overheated and, oh yes, one more thing. No swimming until the blisters have entirely cleared away."

Nadine stopped dead still on the path. "No swimming!" she yelped. "Why I've got to swim. I've got to practice for sports day. I always win the swimming honors for our cabin."

"I'm sorry, Nadine. Really sorry," Miss Molly said, "but there's to be no swimming for either of you."

Miss Molly left them then and the two girls trudged along in silence. Jenny wouldn't have been surprised at anything Nadine had to say to her. She wouldn't have blamed her either. The situation had been bad enough before they'd heard about the no swimming rule. Even so, Jenny had been thinking up a proper apology to offer. Now, however, it was plain that no words she could manage to say would help in the least.

Two of the girls from Indian Village were coming down the path. They stopped and looked at Nadine's and Jenny's white smeared arms. "Why, Nadine, what's the matter?"

"Poison ivy," Nadine said, "and it's all the fault of the Fire Maker here."

"Fire Maker?" Both of the girls turned and looked at Jenny.

To her embarrassment and dismay Nadine began to tell about the whole unfortunate trail hike of the day before. Nadine was a good storyteller and Jenny would have enjoyed the tale except that it was about her. Nadine related the clanking utensils, the picking of the poison ivy for their nature notebooks and then she made a big thing about Jenny's believing that she had to rub two sticks together to start the camp cooking fire.

The older girls said apologetically to Jenny, "Oh, we shouldn't laugh," but they did and after they had gone on down the path they met other girls. Jenny saw them nod back at her and then heard the words, "Fire Maker."

Jenny thought dismally that this was the very way in which a nickname began to fasten itself upon a person.

8

Christmas in July

I⊤ was a hot summer. Everyone said it was the hottest June at Camp Tanda that they could remember and July, of course, was even hotter than June. At breakfast, on the day that the thermometer soared to a new high, Miss Holly said that she had a very special announcement to make.

The girls who had rolled up their shirt sleeves as far as possible and even turned up cuffs in their shorts, now wiped their steaming faces with their napkins and waited for the announcement.

"Tonight," Miss Holly said, "will be Christmas Eve."

"Christmas Eve!" they shouted after her. They couldn't help it. It was such a shock.

"Yes," Miss Holly said. "All regular activities planned for the day will be postponed so that we can use the time to get ready for the Christmas party. The Village girls will take charge of the evening program. The Sunny Glade girls can cut and trim the Christmas tree and the girls from Happy Valley can decorate the lodge. Oh—and there will be presents, of course, and Santa Claus—"

At this point Miss Holly had to stop talking for everyone else was talking, too. Jenny had never seen so many excited people. She felt pretty excited herself.

As they trooped out they passed a box full of paper slips. Each girl took one. On the paper was the name of the camper to whom she would give a present.

Back at Seven Stripe cabin Miss Bugs explained more about it. The presents were to be made by the girls themselves and out of materials which they would find around the camp. On Jenny's slip was written "Marilyn Craig." "She's one of the Indian Village girls," Carol told Jenny and she felt dismayed. Whatever could she find to make that would be an acceptable present for one of the grown-up Village girls?

"Oh you'll think of something," Carol said encouragingly but Jenny didn't feel as confident as Carol.

There were seven cabins in the glade. It was decided that the campers of five of them would go to work on building a stand for the tree and making the decorations. The girls in Miss Bugs' cabin and Miss Connie's next door would climb to the pine forest to select the tree and Mr. Willie, the camp caretaker, would drive up in the truck to bring the tree back.

"All right, let's get going," Miss Bugs said. "Jenny, don't forget to put on the proper shoes."

"Oh, I won't," Jenny said and pulled a white sock over the adhesive patch on her heel and then laced up the oxfords.

This time they climbed even higher than they had gone on the cook-out hike but Jenny, who had been hiking or climbing every day since she had come to camp, didn't feel in the least tired.

It was shady and cool in the pine tree forest. The biggest trees stood so close together that they made a roof and no sky showed through. It was dark and very quiet. "Everyone sit down," Miss Connie said, "and smell and listen." Miss Connie was the dramatics director and liked to have the girls "experience things."

Jenny dropped down on the deep ground covering of fallen pine needles which were as soft and comfortable as her bed at home. Everyone had stopped talking and it seemed to Jenny that the roar of the wind in the top of the pines was like a train coming closer and then fading away. At any rate she had heard the sound of the wind in the pines described in such a fashion. Of course there really wasn't a wind today. Just a small breeze.

All of a sudden June flung herself down full length and stretched out her arms. In a high, breathless voice she said, "Isn't it lovely here? So sweet and peaceful. I wish I could lie here forever and smell and listen."

Jenny looked at June in astonishment and Carol leaned over to whisper. "It's okay. She isn't sick or nutty or anything. It's just that Miss Connie is getting ready to choose the girls for parts in Robin Hood, the next camp play, and June is crazy to get the part of Maid Marion."

"Why doesn't she just ask Miss Connie?"

"She has. Lots of times. But she doesn't want to pass up any opportunities to let Miss Connie see how dramatic she is."

June was still lying on the ground flailing her arms about. "For heaven's sake, June," Miss Connie said, "sit up. Your hair is full of pine needles and I think you're on top of an ant hill."

Miss Bugs jumped up. "Now to get the tree." They all scrambled to their feet and followed her. "We can take any of the ones marked with red paint," she told them. "The red painted ones are marked for thinning out the forest."

"They're all so big," Sally said, looking up. "Why, they're big enough for telephone poles."

"There are smaller ones at the edge of the forest," Miss Connie said.

"We don't want to get one that is too small," Miss Bugs argued. "The lodge is high, you know. And we want the tree to touch the ceiling."

After a good deal of discussion they decided on the perfect tree and cut it down and dragged it to the narrow rutted roadway where Mr. Willie was waiting with the truck.

He took one look. "Great leaping lizards," he said. "Where do you think you're going to put that? In Rockefeller Center?"

Jenny, who had been taken down to see the enormous Christmas tree in Rockefeller Center practically every year of her life, thought this remark very funny and laughed out loud. No one else did, though. Mr. Willie turned and gave Jenny a very pleased smile. She had the feeling that she had just made a new friend.

Mr. Willie loaded the tree and the girls hurried back the way they had come. Because their path was straight down the hill they reached the lodge before the truck did. The papooses from Happy Valley were happily decorating the inside. They had cut icicles and snowflakes of white paper and were pasting them over the windows. They squealed merrily when the Christmas tree was carried in.

"Careful, everyone," Miss Bugs called out. "Set it down—easy—easy. That's it. Now straighten it up." Miss Bugs was on her knees at the base of the tree. She could hardly be seen through the thick branches. Even her voice seemed rather muffled. "Straighten it up," she called again.

There was a little silence. Miss Bugs called more loudly. "Why don't you straighten it up? Can't anyone hear me?"

"We can hear you all right, Bugs," Miss Connie said. "But we can't straighten up the tree. It's about four feet too tall."

All the girls were giggling. Miss Bugs crawled out and looked at the tree with exasperation just as if it had had no business in getting so tall. "Too tall is it!" Miss Bugs snorted. "Well, I'll soon fix that. Someone get me the saw."

Just then one of the little girls stepped into a bucket of flour and water paste and everyone rushed over to fish her out and clean up the mess.

"Now," Miss Bugs called to them. "Now the tree will straighten up all right." She was pushing it into position herself.

"Oh, oh," Carol shouted. "Look what Miss Bugs has done!"

"What I've done," Miss Bugs said, "is to cut off this tree so that it will fit the lodge."

"But, Miss Bugs, you've cut off the top instead of the bottom."

They all looked up. Sure enough the top of the tree was gone. It lay on the floor beside the saw. "Now however could I have made a mistake like that?" Miss Bugs said in astonishment. They were all laughing.

The little papooses sat down on the floor and simply shrieked.

Just then Miss Holly appeared in the doorway and everyone looked around at everyone else, not sure whether to keep on laughing or take a more serious view of the situation. Miss Holly looked at the tree. "What a novel idea," she said. "How very clever. The tree looks as if it were growing right out through the roof."

"Oh yes," Miss Bugs said modestly, "I am rather clever about things like this." And now the girls really did laugh.

"Well, that's our part of the Christmas decorating done," June said. "Now to get busy with our presents. Any ideas, Jenny?"

"Not yet."

"Come on up to the cabin. We'll look around and see what we can find."

"You go ahead," Jenny said. "I'm going down to the mail cabin first."

"I hope you get something."

"I do, too." Jenny hurried down the path slapping every tree trunk that grew along the way. If she didn't miss a one, she promised herself, there would be a card waiting for her from her parents. She had had only two so far.

Miss Spud was in the mail cabin, lying on the floor

eating an apple and reading a report. Miss Spud was the swimming instructor and she was given her name because it was said that she'd eat a peck of potatoes at every meal if they'd let her.

Miss Spud called out, "Hi, Fire Maker, I mean— Jenny. Sorry but the mail's not in yet. In fact there may not be any. A bridge is out upstream."

"It doesn't matter," Jenny said, trying very hard to act as if it didn't.

"How's the poison ivy coming?"

"Just fine. Miss Molly says that I can start swimming tomorrow."

"You're luckier than Nadine," Miss Spud said. "She broke out in a new patch this morning. I don't know when she'll get to swim."

"Golly, that's awful."

Miss Spud nodded. "Well, Merry Christmas."

"What!" Jenny's mind was on the problem of Nadine. Then she remembered and laughed. "Oh yes, Merry Christmas to you, too. I must get started working on my present now." She went racing up the path to the cabin.

9

❁

A Perfect Present

WHEN Jenny got back to the cabin all the girls were hard at work. "Any ideas yet?" June asked.

Jenny shook her head.

"You can make what we are if you want to." The girls had gotten foil pie tins and filled them with damp sand. In the sand they were making arrangements of bits of evergreen and pebbles and tiny wildflowers. Sally had even found a snail shell for hers. Jenny admired each one but it was what Nadine was making that really excited her.

Nadine had found a robin's egg, pushed from the nest but still unbroken. It was smooth and of the clearest, brightest blue. Nadine had bits of twigs and straw and she was painstakingly constructing a tiny nest for the egg. She looked up and saw Jenny watching her. "I suppose you'd like to copycat what I'm doing," she said.

"I wouldn't think of it," Jenny replied. She had intended to say something apologetic about Nadine's new patch of poison ivy but this clearly was not the time. "My goodness," she said loftily, "it's really not that I don't have any ideas but that I have so many I don't know which one to decide upon."

"I can just bet," Nadine said scornfully.

Jenny walked through the woods at the back of the cabin. If she could find a willow tree she was all set. Her father had taught her how to make a willow whistle that whistled beautifully. Carefully done it would make a gift good enough for even a Village girl. But there was no willow tree in sight.

Idly she picked up an odd bit of branch and twirled it between her fingers. Most of its bark was gone. It was rather old and shiny like the pieces of driftwood she had gathered along the ocean shore. It was rather pretty, too, and reminded her of something. Finally she remembered. It was the little branch of white coral on the dressing table at home. Her mother used to slip her rings over the tips of the branches where they hung and sparkled.

Jenny decided that it was the very thing. She would make a ring holder for Marilyn Craig. The job took most of the afternoon. She peeled off the remaining bark and sanded and polished the wood. Then she fitted it into a slice of a larger branch, carefully cutting the hole with her jackknife. The base did not please her. It was impossible to get it as smooth and shiny looking as the branch. She carried the ring holder down to the craft shop and gave the base a coat of shellac.

"Oh my," Miss Bugs said when Jenny showed it to her. "Are you sure it will dry in time?"

"It's quick drying shellac," Jenny explained.

"I hope it's quick enough."

The gifts were finished by dinner time. The girls left them in the cabin and went down to the dining hall. There was roast turkey and dressing and cranberry sauce and apple salad. Miss Pink, the camp bugler, sat on a stool at the end of the hall under a red tissue paper bell and blew Christmas carols with only a few mistakes.

For dessert a large plum pudding was carried in on a platter. Over it Miss Spud poured a bottle of lemon extract and set the whole thing ablaze. It was a magnificent sight. Unfortunately, the lemon extract on Jenny's piece had not ignited but soaked into the pudding instead. It gave it a rather violent flavor.

After dinner the girls went back for their gifts. Jenny tested the shellac with a finger. It was scarcely sticky at all. They went into the lodge and sat in three large circles around the great Christmas tree. It was gorgeously decorated with tin can ornaments, pine cones dusted with glitter and aluminum foil stars. Strings of cranberries and popcorn swung from branch to branch.

"It's beautiful," Jenny whispered to Miss Bugs. "I like it ever so much better than a Christmas tree with a top."

The evening's festivities were in the charge of the girls from the Indian Village. They announced a fine program beginning with more Christmas carols and ending with the exchange of gifts. However, there was so much excitement over the gifts and each girl was so eager to present the one that she had made, that it was decided to reverse the program. After a slight delay they heard the jingle of sleigh bells and then Santa Claus, wonderfully stuffed and costumed in red flannel and black oilcloth, pranced in.

"It's Miss Connie," June whispered. "Isn't she darling?"

Santa began to speak but had to stop to remove a mouthful of the fringed cleansing tissues from which his beard had been made. He started over. He brought out a book and announced that before he supervised the distribution of the presents he would read some of *The Christmas Carol.*

Immediately everyone grew restless again. The papooses in the circle closest to the tree could hardly sit still. After the Village girls had had a short argument with Santa he agreed to save the reading until later and get on with the present exchange.

After each girl's name was read, Santa said, she and the girl who had a gift for her would come forward to the tree. The first names were called. Now it was really exciting. Everyone wanted to see and kept pushing closer and closer to the tree so that Santa was kept busy pushing them back.

Jenny's heart beat fast. She wanted Marilyn's name to be called and yet she dreaded it, too. When Santa did say "Marilyn Craig" he had to repeat it twice before Jenny could stand up and make her way through the girls to the Christmas tree. Holding the ring holder before her she edged to the center of the lodge. Marilyn was already there. "How very pretty," she said. She reached out for it and Jenny drew it back an instant. "Hold onto the top instead of the base," she whispered. "The shellac isn't quite dry."

Marilyn took it carefully. "How very pretty," she said again.

"It's a ring holder," Jenny explained.

"Oh, of course, a ring holder," Marilyn said enthusiastically. "I've never owned a ring holder. How useful it will be. Thank you very much."

Jenny went back to her place, fairly floating over the girls. The present had been a real success.

Scarcely had she sat down when her own name was called and once more she made her way forward. When she reached the tree one of the very smallest of the papooses was waiting for her. "Here's your present," she said breathlessly, holding out a rectangle made of four twigs lashed together at the corners. "It's coming apart a little but you can fix it easily." The little girl's cheeks were quite pink. She looked pleased and anxious all at the same time.

Jenny took the little object. Whatever could it be? "It's very nice," she said, smiling at the child. "Thank you very much."

"You can put a picture in it," the little girl said happily.

"Oh, a little picture frame," Jenny exclaimed. "Just what I need. It was so nice of you to make it for me."

She took the frame back and showed it to Carol. "Honestly, did you ever see such a cute little girl? I bet she worked awfully hard on this."

After all the gifts were distributed the girls were able to settle down. The Villagers passed around boxes of chocolates. Jenny was astonished when the box offered to her turned out to be the very one Uncle Fred had bought her in Chicago. "Then they weren't eaten up by the people in the office, after all."

"What?" Miss Bugs asked.

"Nothing."

Miss Connie, abandoning the beard, read her story and then they all sang carols. Jenny had the strangest feeling. She remembered that it was July, of course, and that she was far from her home. But still, the smell of the Christmas pine, the glittering of the ornaments, the light reflecting on the windows with their snowflakes and icicles, and most of all the singing of the old loved songs gave her—for just an instant—that almost unbearably wonderful feeling of the moment of Christmas.

"Jenny," it was Miss Holly who had come to kneel down beside her, "the mail arrived and here's a real Christmas surprise for you." It was a letter, a thick letter, addressed in her mother's round, evenly-spaced handwriting.

"Oh, golly," Jenny said and her hands closed on the envelope.

"Open it right now," Miss Holly advised. "I wouldn't wait another minute if I were you."

Jenny didn't. Inside were four big pages covered with her mother's writing and all the margins full of her father's funny little drawings. Between each of the pages was a surprise. There was a pressed flower of brilliant blue which her mother had picked on a mountain top, a dozen bright foreign stamps and a length of ribbon woven in a design of flowers and birds.

Under her pillow, when Jenny went to sleep that unexpected Christmas night, was the letter and the little picture frame.

10

Robin Hood Jenny

EACH of the cabins in turn supplied the wood for the nightly camp fire. Today it was the job of Seven Stripe cabin. The girls and Miss Bugs went to the edge of the woods where Mr. Willie had dragged some small trees from land he was clearing. Each girl took a hand with the saw. It was hard going. When it was Miss Bugs' turn she worked away until she was red in the face. "Honestly," she said, "this saw is so dull it would be a lot easier to just chew the logs apart with our teeth."

"I'll go and ask Mr. Willie for a sharper one," Jenny volunteered at once.

"I wouldn't expect you to do that," Miss Bugs said,

wiping her face with the end of her blouse. "His house is half a mile from here."

"Oh, I wouldn't mind in the least." Jenny jumped up and started back along the path. She was pleased to have an excuse for visiting Mr. Willie. Several times when he had asked for campers to help him with unloading supplies, Jenny had volunteered. They had become good friends but Jenny had never visited his house although she had heard a good deal about it from the other girls. In his youth, it was said, Mr. Willie had lived for awhile with the Indians in a wigwam. Now he lived with his sister in a log cabin and looked after Camp Tanda winter and summer.

Jenny passed the Indian Village trying to see as much as she could but still keeping at a safe distance. Only last week three of the Sunny Glade girls had daringly ventured inside the forbidden stockade and come out with their faces painted with Indian stripes.

Jenny paused to watch two of the Villagers who were at archery practice. How strong and tall they stood. How smartly they fitted their arrows and bent their bows. Both arrows struck the target almost in the center. Jenny sighed with admiration. The girls saw her then and waved, "Hi, Fire Maker," they called.

"Hi," she called back. Everyone called her that

now. In fact, except for Miss Bugs and the girls in Seven Stripe cabin, few seemed to remember that her name was Jenny.

Mr. Willie was sitting on the steps of his cabin oiling some tools when Jenny came up the path.

"Great galloping goldfish," he said. "Look who's here."

"I've come to borrow a saw, Mr. Willie." By peering over his shoulder Jenny could see inside the dim cool looking cabin. There seemed to be all sorts of gear and equipment hanging on the walls.

"I've got just what you want," Mr. Willie said, pulling himself erect with a grunt. "Come on in."

This was just what Jenny was hoping to do, so she followed him quickly up the steps and across the wooden porch.

Inside the cabin was simply splendid. All the furniture was made of timbers lashed together with leather. In a second room a woman, older even than Mr. Willie, was sitting at a table peeling potatoes. She didn't turn around when they came in. Mr. Willie went close to her. "Sister Kate, here's company. Here's the Fire Maker."

She cupped a hand to her ear. "What did you say?"

Mr. Willie shouted, "I said the Fire—"

"Fire! Fire!" the old lady screeched. "Where's the fire?" She jumped up and began running around the kitchen, looking in the pans on the stove and out the window.

Mr. Willie charged after her. "No, no," he shouted, "I mean here's company."

Sister Kate stopped and saw Jenny. "Sit right down, dear," she said, "and tell me your name. Mr. Willie is so busy playing tricks he's forgotten his manners."

"Jenny."

"Louder, dear."

"JENNY."

"Oh, Benny! How unusual. But I know it's fashionable these days for girls to have boys' names."

Mr. Willie smiled at Jenny and gave a helpless little shrug. "The saw is in the back room. I'll get it."

When he returned Jenny was looking at the corner where a fishing creel and a bear trap were hanging side by side. "Mr. Willie," she said, "do you know how to make a fire without using matches?"

"I reckon I do." Mr. Willie sat down at the table across from Jenny and lit his pipe. "And many's the time I've had reason to be glad of it."

Jenny leaned forward. "How do you do it?"

"Several ways," Mr. Willie said thoughtfully. From the wall he took down a crude short bow and a board with a notched hole in it. "This is the rubbing stick way. Caught in a pinch a good woodsman could make up a set like this and get a fire going. But it's a long and tricky business and takes a lot of experience."

"Do you think I could learn to do it, Mr. Willie?" Jenny asked, leaning forward. "If I worked very hard do you think I could do it?"

Mr. Willie sucked on his pipe and looked hard at Jenny. "Probably not," he said at last.

"Oh," she said. "Oh. Well, it doesn't really matter. It was just an idea I had. My goodness, we've certainly got plenty of matches up at the camp."

Mr. Willie apparently hadn't heard her. He seemed lost in thought. "But now there's another way of making fire," he said, "with flint and steel. I think it's quite possible you might manage that. With a lot of work and practice, of course."

"I'd work and practice all the time," Jenny promised eagerly. "Every chance I got."

From the wall Mr. Willie took down a small, old leather bag fastened with thongs. From it he took a broken file, a small rock, a mass of fuzzy looking stuff and something that looked like burned paper.

"The steel," he said, putting his finger on the file, "and this rock is flint." He picked up the fuzzy stuff. "Shredded red cedar bark. The very best tinder there is. And this is charred cloth. Now come outside with me and I'll show you how it's done."

Jenny knelt beside him. He arranged some of the tinder in a small nest on a piece of shingle and put a bit of the charred cloth in the center. Then holding the steel close to the cotton he struck the flint downward against it, time after time, and the small sparks rained onto the cotton. Finally there was a tiny wisp of smoke, then a smolder and a glow. Mr. Willie knelt quite close and began to fan and blow. All of a sudden the tinder burst into flame.

"Mr. Willie," Jenny exclaimed, "I never saw anything so wonderful in all of my life."

"Come now," Mr. Willie said. "It isn't so wonderful as all that." But he looked very pleased. "You want to try?"

Jenny was so eager to try that she was quivering. Mr. Willie made another little nest of red cedar tinder and put charred cloth in the center. Then he handed the flint and steel to Jenny. Kneeling as Mr. Willie had done, Jenny struck the steel again and again. "You're holding it too high," he said. "Now it's too low. Great hiccuping horses, you've practically got your nose in the tinder."

Jenny tried and tried. She got sparks from the steel but they didn't seem to hit the cloth. Or if they did nothing came of it. She grew hot and her back felt as if it was breaking in two. But she kept on trying.

"I think you're working too hard at it," Mr. Willie said. "Let me show you once more." This time with little trouble he had a brisk fire blazing away.

Sister Kate came to the door of the cabin. "Willie," she said tartly, "it seems that today you've got fire on your brain."

Grinning at Jenny, Mr. Willie pulled himself to his feet and stamped out the little blaze. Then he replaced the fire making materials in the leather bag and tightened the drawstring. He held the bag out to Jenny. "Take it along. Do some practicing. You'll get the knack."

"Oh, could I? Would you let me?" Jenny faltered, not believing that such a marvelous thing could happen to her. "I mean, won't you need it?"

"I reckon not," Mr. Willie said. "We've got plenty of matches, too." With a wink at Jenny he shouted to Sister Kate, "We've got matches, haven't we?"

"Yes, we have," the old lady shouted back, "and you're not going to get your hands on a one of them."

"Goodbye, Miss Kate," Jenny called.

"Goodbye, Benny. You come again, dear, and we won't have any more of this fire nonsense. I'll show you all my fancy work."

On her way back to camp Jenny thrust the small bag into her pocket. Her pockets were always bulging out oddly and one new bulge wouldn't be noticed.

When she reached the place where the fallen timber was piled she found no one. All the wood for the evening campfire was sawed and stacked. This was fortunate for it wasn't until then that Jenny remembered that she had forgotten to bring along the sharp saw. Probably everyone was now at Miss Connie's tryouts for Robin Hood.

Whistling gaily, Jenny hurried to the clearing where play practices were held. It was next to Miss Connie's cabin. Ducking under a line of wet towels and bathing suits, Jenny saw all the girls seated in a group and Miss Connie in front of them holding a book and talking in a rather pleading voice.

"Now, girls, please settle down. Stop whispering. June, stop smirking and waving your arms around. I can't believe that Maid Marion ever behaved in such a fashion."

Jenny sat down at the edge of the group. She had no idea of trying out for the play but it would be fun watching the others. She put her arms around her knees and rocked happily back and forth. She felt like the king of the world. She felt as if she had a million dollars in that little bag in her pocket.

"Girls," Miss Connie was saying, "there must be some of you who are good at archery. Robin Hood must be the very best. Now will the girls who are really good archers please step forward?"

It was plain that most of the girls considered themselves good archers but no one wanted to be the first
to move forward. "Please, girls," Miss Connie urged.

Nadine was sitting next to Jenny and poked her
with her elbow. "Go on," she said sarcastically.
"Why don't you step forward? You're so good at
everything else. I bet you're just wonderful at
archery."

Jenny was going to say that she had never held a
bow in all her life but then thought, why bother to
explain that to old Nadine? She got up to move to
another place. Suddenly Miss Connie pounced on her
and thrust a bow and arrow into her hands. "Good,

here's one girl who isn't too shy to show what she can do. Good for you, Jenny."

"Good for you, Jenny," Nadine snickered. "Go on and show what you can do."

What Jenny thought she would like to do was to crack Nadine over the head with the bow. She stood considering for a moment. The bow felt rather good in her hands. Archery couldn't be too hard. Certainly the Village girls she had seen that morning seemed to do it easily enough. Besides today was her lucky day. She stood straight and tall as she had seen the older girls do.

"Good," Miss Connie said. "Oh, very good."

Carefully, Jenny placed the arrow against the string of the bow.

"The other end," June whispered and Jenny turned the arrow around. She raised the bow and pulled back on the string, but before she had quite faced the target the string snapped away from her and the arrow went zinging out into space.

There was one loud, long yell from the group.

"Where is it," Jenny asked excitedly. "Where did it go, Miss Connie? Did I send the arrow through the target?"

Miss Connie was clutching her hair. "Jenny," she said in a tone of great anguish, "you sent that arrow right through my bathing suit."

11

A Homesick Papoose

THE second session of Camp Tanda had begun. Some of the campers had gone home and new girls had come to take their places. Of the original group in Seven Stripe cabin only Carol and Nadine and Jenny remained. June had returned to Star Center and Sally to her parents' ranch in Colorado. It seemed very strange without them. Miss Bugs was away, too. Her grandparents were having their golden wedding anniversary and Miss Bugs was spending a week helping them celebrate it.

It rained almost every day and Jenny had not heard from her parents for two weeks because they were camping in the high mountains in Austria. Worst of all Jenny seemed to have a strange illness.

Every night when taps blew the sickness started. First a hard lump in her throat and then a horrid feeling in her stomach. She had to lie quietly on her cot for Miss Laurel who was taking Miss Bugs' place wanted everything perfectly quiet after taps. Jenny couldn't tell Miss Laurel about her sickness before taps because it never started until after taps. Besides she didn't know Miss Laurel very well and felt rather shy with her.

So she just had to lie there. She didn't even have Carol to whisper to for she had been moved to the end of the cabin and new girls had the beds on either side of Jenny.

She decided to go and see Miss Holly. Her mother had said, "If you ever need help go to Miss Holly." Jenny felt that she certainly did need help. Her parents wouldn't want her to be sick with them so far away on that mountain top in Austria. My goodness, when her mother heard about it she would probably get right on that plane and come and see what was the matter. Her mother would probably be glad to come home by this time, anyway. She didn't like traveling nearly so well as her father did.

The path to Miss Holly's little house went down around back of the kitchen and dining hall. Miss Holly was writing in a book. She laid down her pen.

"Jenny, how nice of you to come and see me. I've

been hoping you would. But I know how busy you girls in Seven Stripe cabin are."

"We're not so busy now," Jenny said. "Most of the girls are new and we don't know each other very well yet and Miss Bugs is away celebrating with her grandparents and it's rained so much we can't even work on the requirements for the camp craft honor."

"Well," Miss Holly said, "have you had a letter from your parents lately?"

"Not for two weeks," Jenny said. "They're up on some mountain. My mother doesn't like mountains very much."

Miss Holly nodded. "Neither do I. Whenever I come to one of those sharp hairpin turns on the side of a mountain I always feel that there won't be anything around the corner except empty air. It's silly, of course, but that's what comes of being mid-westerners like your mother and me."

"I'm an easterner," Jenny said. She sat a little straighter. "Miss Holly what I wanted to talk to you about was this sickness."

"Are you sick, Jenny?"

"Not right now. Just in the night."

"Every night?"

"Every night this week."

"Where is the pain?"

"It's not a pain exactly. It's this funny feeling. In

my throat and then in my stomach and then—"

She was interrupted by a kind of alternate hiccuping and sobbing that seemed to be growing louder.

"It's little Mary Peachem back again," Miss Holly said and went to open the screen door. "Come in, Mary."

A very bedraggled little girl came into the room, sniffing and wiping her eyes. Her cheeks were splotched with tears and the front of her shirt looked as if she'd been in a sprinkler.

"Here's my book," she said between sniffles. "I brought it the way you told me." She held out a very grubby looking folder with "Wildflowers" printed on it and underneath "Mary Peachem" in scattered, wobbly letters of different sizes.

"Thank you, Mary." Miss Holly took the folder and looked at it with interest. She said to Jenny, "Mary is one of the new girls in Happy Valley but she's decided not to stay at Camp Tanda."

"I can't," the little girl sobbed. "I have to go home. I know my mother is lonesome for me." Jenny looked up at Miss Holly and smiled but Miss Holly was quite serious.

"Mary had planned to go home at once but we decided that it would be a shame for her not to first finish her present for her mother. She has made this booklet and now she is going to gather wildflowers to press between each of the pages."

"And write their—their names underneath," Mary added with a gulp.

"And write their names underneath," Miss Holly agreed. "I had planned to go with Mary and help her find the flowers but now I think I have a better idea. Why don't you two girls go together? Jenny, you've been here long enough to know where all the best places are."

The idea of taking this miserable little girl out into the woods and helping her search for flowers didn't appeal to Jenny in the least. She considered how she might say so without appearing to seem rude.

Mary, however, had no concern with appearances. She didn't want to go with Jenny and she came right out and said so. She looked as if she was going to start weeping again.

"Well, my goodness," Jenny said. "I don't see why you feel that way about going with me. I know all kinds of places where beautiful wildflowers are growing. I know some secret paths to get to them, too."

"Oh, it is a pity that you aren't going to go with Jenny," Miss Holly said. "What a fine trip you would have had."

Mary changed her mind. With Jenny in the lead they started off. "Where are the wildflowers?" she demanded. "Where are the secret paths?"

Jenny looked around a little anxiously. Where, indeed, were those flowers and paths? "You will have to be patient," she said with dignity. "We haven't come to them yet."

A tree had fallen across the trail and Jenny swung in a wide circle around it. There, growing beside a rock, was a cluster of tiny pink flowers.

"Oh, you did find them," Mary said. She knelt down.

"Just pick one," Jenny said. "Leave the others to make seed." That was one of the things Miss Pink had told them just the other day. Thank goodness, she had been listening.

"Of course," Mary said respectfully. She picked one and held it up. "What kind of a flower is it?"

Jenny took it and looked at it closely. As far as she could see it was a tiny pink flower. "Do you know what I think would be a good idea?" she said to Mary. "I think it would be a good idea if we gather the flowers and take them back and let Miss Holly help with the naming of them when you put them in the folder. Because if you found out the names now you might get mixed up later."

This seemed like a very good idea to Mary. They kept on looking and found yellow flowers, a feathery red one and a light blue that Jenny identified positively as wild aster. She told this to Mary several times. "I do wish we could find some Indian paintbrush," she said, peering beneath the shrubs. "Miss Pink says it grows around here."

"What does it look like, Jenny?"

"Well, sort of bright and Indiany and like a paintbrush." She left the trail again and led the way to a tiny waterfall in the brook. She sat down on a rock. "Let's rest awhile."

Mary sat down beside her. "You found the secret path, too," she said with satisfaction.

There was a willow growing beside the brook.

Jenny took out her pocket knife and cut off a switch. "If you weren't going home so soon," she said, "I'd make you a little willow whistle."

"Couldn't you make it now?"

"No, we have to start back in a minute."

"Couldn't you make it while I'm pressing the flowers in my book?"

"I don't think so," Jenny said. "It has to be done very slowly and carefully."

"Oh." Then Mary added, "It must be nice to be an older girl."

"Do you mean me?" Jenny asked in surprise.

Mary nodded.

"Some day you'll be one, too," Jenny promised. She sat very straight and tall. "Come, dear," she said, "Miss Holly will be wondering where we are."

When they reached the little house, Miss Holly took the flowers. "What a fine collection. You have done very well." She lifted the red feathery looking flower. "Indian paintbrush!" she exclaimed. "Miss Pink said there was some growing around here but this is the first I've seen. You're certainly going to have a splendid gift for your mother, Mary."

Mary looked at the willow switch Jenny still carried. "I'm not going to be able to give the present to my mother as soon as I thought," she said. "Jenny is going to make me a whistle and it is very hard to do and may take a long time, Jenny says."

"Then you'll be staying with us for awhile longer," Miss Holly said. "I'm so glad. You know," she added, "for a surprise the girls in Happy Valley are having a strawberry ice cream party this afternoon and if you hurry I think you will be in time for it."

Jenny and Miss Holly watched the little girl speed down the path, the flowers and the notebook clutched in her arms.

"She was homesick, wasn't she?" Jenny asked.

"Terribly," Miss Holly said. "Especially at night. But I have a feeling that she is going to be all right after this."

Jenny sat silently for a moment. "I don't suppose a person could be homesick after quite a while, could she?" she asked. "I mean a person would be feeling just fine for weeks and then suddenly she would be homesick?"

"That's the very way it worked with me," Miss Holly confided. "The first time I'd ever been away from home was when I went off to college. I was fine for about two months and then this homesickness hit me. Usually in the night but sometimes even in the day. There was a hard tight feeling in my throat and an awful feeling in my stomach."

Jenny nodded and leaned forward. "What did you do about it?"

Miss Holly sighed. "I really hoped you wouldn't ask me that for I'm not very proud of the way I behaved. I wept and wailed and made everyone around me perfectly miserable. And I was much too old. You can expect such behavior from a little girl but an older girl should try to manage better."

"What should she do?"

"I would say, keep busy and think of all the happy things she can and try not to feel sorry for herself and to remember especially that homesickness finally does go away. Oh, it's not easy, I know. It takes real courage to conquer homesickness."

"My mother says that I have so much courage that it almost worries her," Jenny said.

Miss Holly looked at the willow switch. "I know it's a lot to ask, but when you've finished the whistle for Mary, do you suppose you could make me one? It's something I've always wanted."

"Of course," Jenny said, jumping up. "I'll make you a dandy. I'll go back and get another switch right now."

She ran so fast that it was only a few minutes until she got back to the tree growing beside the little brook. After she had selected and cut a fine piece for Miss Holly's whistle she was still so out of breath that she sat down again on the rock. She took out the little leather bag that she always carried with her and looked at the fire making materials. She had tried many times but she hadn't yet succeeded in getting a flame. This would be a good time to practice.

Carefully she cleared an area of all leaves and twigs as she had been instructed by Mr. Willie and in camp craft class. Then she arranged the tinder and put a bit of charred cloth on it. Carefully holding the file she struck the stone against it. Sparks fell onto the cloth and there was a wisp of smoke and finally a small flame. Jenny jumped to her feet with a great shriek. She had done it. She had made fire! It was burning well now. She hated to do it but she stamped the fire out and then covered the spot with handfuls of damp earth.

She heard a crackling along the path and Miss Bugs crashed into view. "What is it?" she said. "I heard this terrible yell and—"

"Miss Bugs. You're back. It's really you!"

"You recognize me," Miss Bugs cried in a dramatic voice. "I've been gone a whole week and you still know who I am."

They laughed together and went up the path to Seven Stripe cabin. That night the beds were shuffled around again. Miss Laurel had gone and Miss Bugs said she didn't care where they slept as long as they kept quiet and let her sleep. So the two new girls moved together and Carol came back by Jenny.

"Good night," she whispered in the dark.

In the quiet of the cabin Jenny lay and thought. It had been such an exciting day. First of all there was the matter of the fire. She had been tempted to tell Miss Bugs but she wanted to keep it a secret until she had practiced a lot and could do it every time. Then there were the whistles she was going to make. She would whittle carefully and do good work—especially on Miss Holly's.

The long slow notes of taps sounded out across the camp. It was time for the homesickness to begin. Jenny braced herself. She remembered that Miss Holly had said to think about happy things, try not to feel sorry for herself. All right, she was ready. Let the sickness come. She waited and she waited. Nothing happened. In fact she felt wonderful. She fell asleep.

12

Danger on the Rocks

THE second half of the summer session of Camp Tanda seemed to be going by in a flash. The annual sports day was held and Jenny brought honor to Seven Stripe cabin by winning second place in the free style swimming race. Nadine was third. The girls in Indian Village staged a Pow Wow and invited the entire camp. In their paint and beaded costumes the girls performed the Chippewa scalp dance and the Pueblo Comanche dance. Watching them in the flashing light of the camp fire Jenny had gotten so excited that the back of her neck prickled.

The weather was fine again and everyone who was trying for the camp craft honor was busy. It was the most difficult honor to earn and the most desired.

At the grand council fire that closed each session of Camp Tanda Miss Holly presented to each girl who had successfully completed the requirements, a silver pin in the form of a tiny woodsman's ax. Jenny yearned for such a pin.

She had passed her safety tests, slept for three successive nights with the stars for a roof, hiked five miles packing necessary food and cooking gear, learned the ropes and lashings and demonstrated how to build a wet weather fire.

In Seven Stripe cabin the girls were packing for one last climb up Tomkins's hill to finish their camp craft requirements. This time they would go over the top of the hill to the rock ledges and cook their lunch there in a reflector oven which they would construct. "Cherry pies, among other things," Miss Bugs said happily.

It was Jenny's job to carry the rather large and bulky cans of cherries. "Why don't we make pies out of something else?" she suggested.

Miss Bugs looked interested. "For instance—what?"

Jenny considered. "I could search for berries in the woods. I think that would be fun."

The girls groaned. "We'd starve to death before Jenny found enough berries to feed us." In the end Jenny loaded up the cans and they set off. Miss Laurel and the girls in her cabin went with them.

Crossing the top of Tomkins's hill was almost like crossing into another country. A steep path descended into a little valley. From the meadow there, a series of ledges rose, one upon another, up and up until they made a mountain of their own.

"Imagine trying to climb a thing like that," Carol said.

"Some boys from the camp across the river did once," Nadine told them. "But I guess no girl ever did."

Carol shook her head. "I sure wouldn't try. That's the biggest pile of rock I've ever seen."

"In Austria, where my parents are, the mountains are thousands of feet high. My mother and father climb them all the time." Jenny studied the sheer faced rock. She could see tiny crevices and flat spots that would give a toe hold. "My goodness," she said, "my father could climb that—and so could I."

"I just bet," Nadine said with a scornful snort. "You'd get two feet off the ground and be scared to death."

"If any one of you gets two feet or even one of your feet up the side of that ledge," Miss Bugs threatened, "I'll personally scare you to death. You all know the rules. Climbing over there is absolutely forbidden."

Miss Laurel came hurrying over. "Bugs, if we're going to get those pies baked, we must get the reflector oven put together and the girls haven't even started on it yet and—"

"Okay, okay," Miss Bugs said soothingly. It was Miss Laurel's first year as a counselor and she hadn't yet learned to relax.

The oven went together rather easily and a fine fire was soon blazing merrily away. The pie dough was more of a problem. Someone put too much water in the first batch and it became a sticky mess. By the time three pies were satisfactorily assembled the fire had burned out and the fuel was almost exhausted. "I'll get more," Jenny volunteered. "I saw some good stuff over at the foot of the ledge."

She had gathered half an armload when she heard the crackling of twigs behind her. A bear perhaps? She whirled around. There stood Nadine. "Honestly," Jenny said, stooping to gather the wood she had dropped in her fright, "honestly, do you have to sneak up on a person like that?"

"I wasn't sneaking," Nadine said, "and even if I was, you've been pretty sneaky yourself lately. And doing some mighty queer things."

"Like what?" Jenny demanded.

"Like pulling bark off trees and burning something up. Your shirt, I think."

So Nadine had been snooping around. "It wasn't a shirt I burned. It was an old handkerchief."

"What for? What did you burn it for, Jenny?"

Jenny looked at Nadine. She had burned the handkerchief because her practicing had used up all the charred cloth Mr. Willie had given her and she had to make more. It was the same with the tinder. Mr. Willie had helped her to find the right tree and shown her how to crush and shred the bark.

"What else did you see, Nadine?"

"Nothing," Nadine admitted reluctantly. "What else was there to see?"

Jenny still planned to keep the whole fire making business a secret until she could do it every time. Certainly she wasn't going to let old Nadine be the first to find out about it.

"What else is there to see?" Nadine repeated.

"It's a secret. You'll find out when the time comes," Jenny said airily and prepared to return to the cooking site with the firewood.

Nadine blocked her path. "Oh, you and your secrets. You're always so smart. You're always saying you know everything and can do everything. Stupid bragging. That's all it is. Like saying you could climb the ledges."

Jenny examined the face of the rock again and saw the small crevices and the narrow ledges that would support a person. "I could climb that. My goodness I've climbed all sorts of rocks with my father."

"I'll just bet," Nadine sneered. "You and that wonderful father of yours. I'll bet he's as much of a scaredy as you are."

Jenny threw the wood away from her so that it fell with a crash and then she approached the ledge. Nadine said nothing. The first ten feet up the side of the rock was simple, Jenny found. One easy foot-hold rose above another. There was a little strip of rock that jutted out. Facing the rock and keeping hold of outcroppings, Jenny edged along. Just as her father had told her, she didn't look down. Not once. It was harder going now. The crevices were farther apart and harder to find. She searched care-fully with her toe for each one before she shifted her weight to it. She was feeling awfully hot, and paused, wishing she could free her hand to wipe the perspiration from her face.

"Don't go any higher, Jenny, come down," Nadine shouted at her, and Jenny turned her head to look down at the girl. Nadine seemed straight below her and so small. Jenny felt as if she were standing on air. She had never climbed anything like this before. Actually she had only climbed small rock outcrop-pings with her father and not very often at that and he had always been right behind her, big and strong, ready with his arm to steady and reassure her.

"Jenny, don't go any higher," Nadine pleaded. "You'll fall. You'll be killed. Come back down."

"I can't." The words came out of Jenny in a little choked sob. "I can't move." It was true. She couldn't make herself move in either direction. She felt as if she were fastened to the rock. "Get somebody, Nadine. Get somebody quick."

She didn't dare look down to see if Nadine had

gone. There was nothing but silence below and it seemed like hours went by and nothing happened except that her arms ached and her fingers felt as if they were clawing right through the rock.

Then someone called softly. It was Miss Bugs. "Hi, mountain goat. Don't move. I'm coming up to get you down. I want to see how the scenery is up there."

With her face still against the rock Jenny couldn't help a small smile. Crazy Miss Bugs. All the girls must have come, too. She could hear them chattering and exclaiming below her.

"Laurel, keep them quiet," Miss Bugs ordered. Jenny closed her eyes and waited and then she heard Miss Bugs quite close. "It's okay, Jenny. Everything's under control. It really wasn't much of a climb. I have a rope. I'm going to make it secure on the rock and tie one end around you. Then you work your way back along the ledge and I'll keep the rope steady and you'll be perfectly safe. There. That's it. Now get going."

Jenny felt the rope around her waist and Miss Bugs' hand on her shoulder. "I can't," she whimpered. "It's as if I were frozen or something. I can't move."

"Of course you can," Miss Bugs said. "And you're going to. Right now!"

Jenny moved out across the ledge and then felt the first firm foothold. The rope was taut around her waist. "Fine, fine," Miss Bugs called to her. "You're doing fine, Jenny."

Then she heard Miss Laurel's voice directly below. "You're almost down. Another two steps and I can reach you." Then Miss Laurel's hands were around her waist and it was only a small jump to the ground.

The girls gave a great whoop. "Quiet, everyone," Miss Laurel ordered. "Do be careful, Bugs," she called and she sounded scared. Jenny looked up. Miss Bugs stood above her on a narrow, narrow shelf of rock.

"It's all right," she called back. "I can make it." As Jenny had done she eased along the ledge, her face to the wall, grasping the outcroppings. She groped for the first foothold, found it and found another. Then she put her foot on a small rock shelf. There was a sharp crack and the shelf gave way. Miss Bugs came falling, sliding down the face of the rock and when she hit the ground she crumpled up into a motionless heap.

"She's dead," someone screamed.

"Stand back," Miss Laurel said. She knelt by Miss Bugs, still motionless and then she got up. Her face was white. "Carol, I'm leaving you here in charge with Jane and Nadine. The rest of you come with me. We're going back to camp for help. Don't touch Miss Bugs." Her voice was firm until she said, "Miss

Bugs" and then it cracked a little.

"Is someone calling me?" Miss Bugs rolled over and looked at them. She rubbed her eyes. "Who hit me over the head and why is everyone staring?"

"Oh Bugs!" Miss Laurel who had been so brave and calm now seemed to go all to pieces. "Bugs, you're all right. I thought—I thought—"

"For heaven's sake, Laurel," Miss Bugs said. "Stop crying. You're dripping all over me." She looked up at Jenny. "Well, we made it, didn't we?"

Miss Laurel looked at Jenny, too. "It's a miracle Bugs wasn't killed trying to save you. Why did you climb on those rocks? You know it was against the rules. You've broken one of the most important laws of camping. Never, deliberately or carelessly, to place yourself or any other person in danger. Miss Holly will certainly not give you the camping award now."

"Hey, Laurel," Miss Bugs said. "Get hold of yourself. All's well that ends well, I always say. But what I want to know is—who is watching those pies? I guess I'd better go do it myself before they're burned to a crisp." She started to get up and let out a yelp and a strange look came on her face. "I guess I've twisted my ankle."

Miss Laurel felt it and Miss Bugs winced. "I'm afraid it's broken, Bugs. Don't move. I'll go to camp for help. Come on girls."

Jenny stood not moving, looking at Miss Bugs, the tears flowing from her eyes.

"Come, Jenny," Miss Laurel said.

"Oh, let the Fire Maker stay with me," Miss Bugs said. "She can bring me my pie when it's baked."

13

Bravery and Bragging

THE next morning Miss Laurel told the girls that
Miss Bugs' ankle was broken, that it had been put in
a cast, and that she was in bed down at the health
lodge. The Seven Stripe cabin girls went down to see
her after breakfast.

The others went in but Jenny held back at the
door. It seemed terrible to think of Miss Bugs, always
so bouncey and gay, lying helpless in bed. And all
Jenny's fault.

Miss Bugs called out, "Hey, where's the Fire
Maker?" and then she went in. Miss Bugs was sitting up in bed with her foot in a huge cast propped
up on a pillow. The girls stood around looking
solemn.

"Oh, boy," Miss Bugs said, stretching her arms over her head. "Is this ever the life? I'm just going to read and eat all day long. I expect to be waited on hand and foot. Especially that foot," she said, pointing to the cast. "And when I get out of here I'm thinking of assigning Jenny and Nadine to carry it as I hop around." The girls began to laugh, even Jenny.

"Now," Miss Bugs said, "I want each of my visitors to write her name on the cast so that I can check up on the ones who don't come to see me. Let's draw slips of paper and see who's first."

In the bustle of preparing the slips Miss Laurel came to the door. "Jenny, Miss Holly wants to see you at her little house."

Everyone was silent as Jenny left. Outside Miss Laurel said, "I got pretty excited and was awfully hard on you yesterday, Jenny. I'm sorry."

"I deserved it," Jenny said. Her throat felt dry. "What—what does Miss Holly want me for?"

Miss Laurel shook her head. "She just said for you to come." Jenny hurried along the path. Maybe she would be put out of camp. Maybe she would be sent home. But there was no one at home. The apartment was all closed up. Even Mike, her goldfish, was staying with the cleaning woman.

Miss Holly was putting papers into a briefcase.

124

Bravery and Bragging

"Come in, Jenny," she said briskly. "I find I have to drive to Star Center today. I thought that since it was the town where your mother grew up, you might enjoy going with me."

Jenny, who had been expecting the worst, was made speechless by this delightful invitation. In a few minutes she found herself sitting beside Miss Holly in a bright blue car and driving out the gate.

Miss Holly, it seemed, wasn't going to talk about what had happened the day before. She was, in fact, talking about things that happened a good many years before. About when the camp was new and Jenny's mother was there.

"Your mother was one of our best campers, Jenny. I believe that she was the bravest girl at Camp Tanda."

"My mother—brave?" Jenny asked in amazement, wondering if Miss Holly hadn't gotten mixed up and was thinking of some other girl.

"Yes, very brave." Miss Holly slowed the car and turned off the highway onto a rutted side road. "It's a little out of the way, but I want to take you to see a certain place and tell you a story."

The place where Miss Holly drove was very beautiful. It was a high overlook. Below them Jenny could see the shining bend of the river. "Why, there's the camp. I can see the buildings through the trees. And there are the swimming pool and the lodge."

"If you look hard you can see the totem pole. When your mother was here, Jenny, we didn't have any of these buildings or the swimming pool."

"I know. Mother has told me. All the girls lived in tents down by the river and at night you all sat together around a camp fire and sang."

"Yes, it was like that." Miss Holly was silent a minute as if she was remembering those days. "Another thing we didn't have was the great dam that controls the river. Has your mother ever told you about the night we had the flash flood?"

"No. I'm sure she hasn't. I would have remembered."

"It was the only time it happened," Miss Holly said, "and we were totally unprepared. It was just after sundown. One minute the tents were on dry land and the next, water was swirling around them. It rose rapidly. We left everything behind and got all of the girls into the hills back of the camp. All of them except two of the smallest who grew panicky and ran away downstream where the ground was low. Your mother was one of the older girls then. She took our canoe and went after them. She found them huddled on a little knoll not yet reached by the water. They were hysterical and refused to get into the canoe. The water was still rising. There was a tree on the knoll, small but large enough to bear the weight of the little girls. Your mother tied them into the branches and that was the way we found them in the morning. Your mother was clinging to the tree. The water was almost to her knees. The children were hungry, shivering with cold but calm. She had sung to them and told them stories all night."

Neither Jenny nor Miss Holly spoke for some time after that. "When Mother found them and they wouldn't get in the canoe, she could have paddled herself to higher ground and been safe, couldn't she?"

"Yes."

"And she didn't know that the water would stop at her knees either. She didn't know how far up it would come." Jenny shuddered as she said it.

"Now you know why I call her our bravest camper."

"But that isn't the way my mother seems to be," Jenny said. "She acts as if she was afraid of things. I always thought she was timid."

"That makes what she did on the night of the flash flood even more courageous, doesn't it? There's a big difference between brave talk and brave action."

"I know," Jenny said very low. "That's the way it was yesterday when Miss Bugs got hurt." Now Jenny wanted to talk about yesterday. She almost felt that she had to. "That's what I was doing, talking brave. I guess what I was really doing was bragging and I said to—I mean I told—"

"It's all right," Miss Holly said. "You needn't worry about mentioning Nadine. I know all about her part in it."

"You do?" Jenny was astonished. "But no one else was there. Just Nadine and me."

"Nadine told me," Miss Holly said. "She came to my house last night and told me the whole story. She said that if you weren't going to get your Camp Craft honor she didn't deserve hers either."

Jenny was even more astonished.

"Oh, I'm aware that Nadine isn't the most popular girl in camp," Miss Holly said, "and with good reason. But I've never known her to do a dishonorable thing."

"No," Jenny agreed, "nothing like that. It's just that she's so sort of—"

"Jenny, did you ever see a chestnut burr?"

Jenny shook her head.

"A chestnut burr has a sharp prickly shell but inside there's a fine sweet nut. I think it's like that with Nadine. On the outside she's prickly but on the inside she—"

Jenny began to laugh and Miss Holly laughed, too. "Oh, dear, dear. I certainly didn't mean to say that Nadine is a nut, even a fine sweet one."

"I think I know what you mean, Miss Holly. If I'd try harder to find something nice about Nadine I probably would."

"Life is pretty wonderful for you, Jenny, and for most of the other girls. You have good homes, parents who watch over and love you. But what if you had no father, a mother whom you seldom saw and who didn't even remember when it was your birthday? And what if you lived with a grandmother who was too old and feeble to give a young girl the guidance and care and love she needed?"

There were tears on Jenny's cheeks. Miss Holly looked over and saw them. She put her arm around Jenny's shoulders and gave a little squeeze. "One of my many faults," she said, "is that, quite often, I say more than I intend to. Well, enough of such talk." She started the engine of the car. "You know, looking at all that water in the river down there has made me very thirsty. You keep a sharp lookout for the first place that sells cold drinks."

It seemed to Jenny that everything in Star Center was exactly the way her mother had told her. In all the years it had stayed the same. Right there in the middle of town was the big gray stone courthouse with the great fir tree on the lawn where each Christmas time the children sang carols and were each given a bag of candy. And there was the schoolhouse.

"Bigger now," Miss Holly said. "It's had two additions." She drove around the block so that Jenny could see her mother's old house. It was painted white and three stories high and had a cupola and two chimneys. There were oak trees on the lawn and a hedge of lilac. It all looked a little shabby and overgrown.

"It's empty now," Miss Holly said. "The last people moved out in the spring." Up the hill from the house was the church. "Behind the church is the coasting hill. In the winter it's covered with sleds. I always thought that was the best place in town."

Jenny looked over at Miss Holly. "Did you go sliding?"

"You bet I did. Belly buster, too."

Miss Holly turned the car around another corner. "I wish I had time to show you more, Jenny, but I must get out home." They turned into a small lane that led up to a rambling house. It had a wide porch and three swings hung from the ceiling by chains. There were a great many chairs, some quite small. Miss Holly said, "You see, in the summer time most people like to read out here. And, of course, in the fall, too, when the weather's fine. It's so handy to the apple orchard."

Jenny couldn't make much of these remarks but Miss Holly had opened the door and Jenny followed her into the house. Inside was even more of a surprise. One room led into another and the walls of each were covered with shelves of books.

Jenny stood in the middle of the biggest room and looked around. "I didn't know anyone owned this many books."

"But I don't own them," Miss Holly began and then interrupted herself. "Jenny, didn't I tell you? This is not only my house, it's the public library."

"The public library!" Jenny sat down. The public library she knew had steep wide steps and stone lions in front and busy attendants and elevators and corridors.

Miss Holly was looking at her rather anxiously. "Well, of course, it isn't a proper library. The town has never had the money to build one but we do have lots of books and people seem to enjoy coming here. See, there's a big fireplace for when it's cold in the winter and the porch is just dandy in the summer and there are lots of places where the school children can study reference material. Well, as I said, it's not a proper library but—"

"I think it's a wonderful library," Jenny said. "I wish I could come here. My goodness, I'd start right in and read every one of those—I mean," she said, feeling her face go red, "I mean I'd certainly like to read some of these books and sit in a swing out there on the porch. My mother told me about almost everything in Star Center but she didn't tell me about the library."

"We didn't have it when she was here. Hello, Grace."

A merry looking woman came bustling through the door. "Oh, it's you, Holly. I couldn't imagine who it was. We had a crowd here this morning but there's a circus at the fair grounds this afternoon and everyone's there."

"Grace, this is Jenny. Jenny, Miss Grace is my partner in the library. It's a very good arrangement. I take care of Camp Tanda in the summer and the library in the winter. Miss Grace has charge of the library while I'm at camp and then in the winter she's at the school. She's the mathematics teacher."

"Oh," Jenny said and tried to sound polite. Mathematics was her very worst subject.

"It's a good arrangement," Miss Grace agreed. "Saturday afternoons all the children who are having trouble with arithmetic can come here and we have a little meeting in the back parlor. We usually pull taffy and pop corn along with our studying and it's amazing how much progress we make."

"That's the nicest way I ever heard of studying arithmetic," Jenny said enthusiastically.

Miss Holly was taking the papers out of her briefcase. "Now I have some business to take care of and I'm going to keep Miss Grace busy, too, for awhile, so you find a book and make yourself comfortable."

"Help yourself to the apples in the dish, dear," Miss Grace said, "and if you take the cover off the plate on the buffet you'll find chocolate cake."

Jenny took an apple and a book and curled up in a big chair. But she didn't eat the apple and she didn't read the book. She sat and daydreamed. Being here in Star Center was like being in a story you knew by heart. She thought of her mother's old house with the lilac hedge, and the children under the Christmas tree on the courthouse lawn and the coasting hill back of the church. She could practically see her mother and Miss Holly sliding down that hill—but what in the world was belly buster?

On the drive home, after a little silence, Miss Holly said, "You understand about the Camp Craft honor, don't you? The awards aren't given by me, you know. They are earned by the girls."

Jenny swallowed. "I understand. I haven't earned the honor."

"But you will," Miss Holly said. "Perhaps next summer."

"Next summer! Do you mean I'll get to come back next summer?" Jenny fairly jumped off the seat in her surprise and excitement.

14

A Secret Shared

As soon as swimming class was over and Jenny had dressed, she raced for the mail cabin. She hadn't had a letter from her parents for three days and that made it pretty sure that there'd be one today. Besides she had promised herself this morning that if she could hop on one foot clear across the swinging bridge on her way to the pool there would absolutely be a letter.

Nadine was in the cabin when Jenny bounced through the door. Miss Spud had finished sorting the mail. She picked up a letter and waved it. "Here you are, Jenny."

"I knew it would be here," Jenny said. She was going to tell about hopping across the bridge on one foot but decided not to with Nadine standing there.

She tore open the envelope. Most of her mother's letters were quite long. This was a short one. They were packing, her mother wrote. They would be flying from Zurich on Friday and would be in New York on Sunday.

Why this was Friday. They were flying today, perhaps this very minute. Jenny glanced up at the sky as if she might see her father and mother swoop overhead. Then she went on with the letter. Miss Holly would make all the arrangements for Jenny, so she needn't concern herself about that. There was, her mother wrote, to be a big surprise for her, but they couldn't tell her about it yet for they didn't quite know themselves.

Jenny flipped over the page and started to read the other side. She heard Nadine speak to Miss Spud.

"You're sure. There isn't anything for me?"

"Sure as sure, Nadine. I looked twice."

"There was such a big pile of mail today. You don't suppose any slipped down behind the counter, do you?"

"Honestly, Nadine!" Miss Spud began, hesitated and finished in a more patient voice. "I don't believe any did. Why don't you come around on this side and help me look?" The two of them poked around under the counter.

Jenny watched. Nadine was looking for a letter

from her mother, of course. The girls said she came down and waited until the mail was sorted every day. If she had ever received a letter from her mother, Jenny hadn't heard about it.

Nadine went out of the mail cabin and Jenny followed her at a short distance. "Nadine," she called. The girl didn't answer or look around but she stopped and Jenny soon came up with her. It was hard trying to be friendly with Nadine but Jenny felt rather as if Miss Holly was pushing her in the back.

"I thought we might walk back to the cabin together," she said.

Nadine shrugged. "I don't care."

They walked side by side in silence. The letter from her mother felt large and conspicuous in Jenny's hand. Almost guiltily she pushed it out of sight into her pocket.

"Getting letters is a pest," Nadine said. "It only means you have to sit down and write an answer. It's all just a pest."

Jenny didn't feel that this was true but it wasn't going to help matters any to say so. Nadine was stalking along never looking at her, so Jenny turned her head and got a quick look at Nadine. The other girl's eyes were sort of wet and she was blinking rapidly. She was crying. Jenny put her hand in the pocket where the letter was and wished with all her heart

that she had the magic to turn it into a letter for
Nadine. Her hand also touched the little leather
pouch that held the fire making materials.

She stopped. "Nadine, I'm ready to tell about my
secret now and if you want I'll show it to you first
of all."

"What do I care about your old secret," Nadine
said but she stopped, too, and looked at Jenny, "Well,
what is it?"

"Follow me," Jenny said mysteriously, and took
a side path until she came to the clearing where she

had so many days practiced her fire making. She began brushing away twigs and leaves. "First we have to clear away a good sized spot so there won't be any danger."

"Go ahead and clear away all you want to," Nadine said. She sat down on a rock. Jenny thought of a very good answer to that but she didn't say it. Making friends with Nadine was about as hard a thing as she had ever tried.

"You're so slow," Nadine complained and she began industriously sweeping away leaves, too.

Jenny took out the pouch and began to lift out her fire making materials. Nadine moved up closer. She watched Jenny arrange the little nest of tinder and place a bit of charred cloth inside. Then she watched her hold the file close to the cloth and strike it with the flint. Now Nadine was on her knees so close to Jenny that their heads almost touched. There were sparks, a thin wisp of smoke and finally a tiny flame which Jenny nursed along into a blaze by adding small twigs. Then she sat back.

Nadine sat back, too, never looking away from the fire. "That's absolutely the most marvelous thing I ever saw," she said slowly.

Jenny was both embarrassed and pleased. She said, "My goodness, that isn't anything. I can do it every —" She stopped. "I've been working and working to do it all summer. I didn't think I'd ever learn how."

"Absolutely the most marvelous," Nadine said again.

Jenny blurted out, "If you like I'll teach you how."

"Jenny, would you really?"

There was a crackle on the path and they both looked up to see one of the Village girls standing there. It was Marilyn to whom Jenny had given the ring holder at the Christmas party. Marilyn looked surprised and worried. "What are you doing with a fire out here?"

"It's perfectly safe," Nadine said. "We took care of that. And this is a very special fire. Jenny made it. Without matches, I mean."

Marilyn dropped down beside them and looked at the small fire burning away. "Did you really, Jenny? I know you're called the Fire Maker but I didn't know you really could."

"Only the two of us know," Nadine said. "Just Jenny and I know the secret."

"Well, you must let me tell the girls in the Village about it," Marilyn said. "It will certainly surprise them. You know we've been trying all summer to do this very thing and not having any luck at all. We wanted so much to make fire to light the blaze at the Grand Council." She stopped and looked at Jenny. "I've a wonderful idea!"

A Secret Shared

Until this point Jenny had not said a word to Marilyn. In the first place she had not expected such enthusiasm from Nadine. Then to have a Villager come along and get excited, too. The whole thing rather unsettled her.

Marilyn said, "Jenny, do you suppose you could light the fire at the Grand Council? The girls would fix an Indian costume for you and you could march into the ring with the Villagers and then, in the center of the ring, make fire. Oh, I can just see it! Do you think you can do it, Jenny?"

Jenny opened her mouth but not a word would come out.

Nadine jumped up. "Can she do it!" she said excitedly. "Of course she can do it. My goodness. Jenny has practiced all summer. She can do it every time."

15

☼

Last Day at Camp Tanda

JENNY wakened long before the first call of the bugle. Light was beginning to streak through the eastern sky. The early morning wind came down from the hills, shaking the dew from the leaves of the trees. From her cot Jenny could see the trees and a patch of sky that was gray slowly turning to blue.

This was the last day of camp. Tonight would be the Grand Council and then in the morning they would pack their things and leave for their homes. The camp would be quite deserted. It was hard to think of it like that.

"Jenny, are you awake?" It was Carol.

"Yes."

"Let's dress and go outside."

Miss Bugs drowsily nodded permission as they slipped out of the cabin. Though it was only past the middle of August there was a nippy feeling in the air and Jenny pulled on her sweater. She said, "Let's walk around and say goodbye to things."

They walked down past the dining hall. There were lights in the kitchen where the cooks were preparing breakfast. They crossed the swinging bridge to the swimming pool. The water glistened clear and blue. They went on to the lodge and sat at the foot of the totem pole. In the meadow the grass had grown long and was beginning to turn to gold.

"If I didn't believe I'd be coming back, I couldn't stand to leave," Jenny said. "It's all so beautiful."

"It's beautiful here in the winter, too. The snow is white and deep. It covers everything and everything looks different."

"Have you ever been here in the winter, Carol?"

"Sure, lots of times. We always come during Christmas holidays for a winter camp. We bring our food and bedrolls and keep a big fire going in the lodge and we hike and skate and ski. Miss Holly brings a whole carload of girls from Star Center."

"It must be exciting to live in Star Center."

Carol considered this. "I suppose really it isn't as exciting as living in a big city but we do have lots of fun. We visit back and forth at each other's homes and there's a fall masquerade and the Christmas bazaar and skating parties. Things like that."

"Do you sing carols under the fir tree on the court-house lawn and get bags of candy and nuts?"

Carol looked surprised. "Yes, we do. Who told you about that?"

"My mother. She sang under that same tree when she was a girl."

"I guess they've done it forever," Carol said. "It's that way in Star Center. Things go on and on and on."

The demanding notes of the bugle swept over the meadow and the girls started back. At the cabin everything was in a scramble.

Above the racket Miss Bugs was trying to issue orders. She clumped up and down the aisle on her cast. "Girls, please get some of your packing done today. And please, please, don't forget anything. The nicest thing you could do for me is to go out of here tomorrow without leaving a dribble of bathing suits, washcloths and teeth retainers. Go to the craft lodge and pick up the things you've made. Go to the nature room and pack your rock and insect collections. Anyone who has medicine or pills at the health lodge go to Miss Holly and check them out. The girls who are to take the Denver train are to meet at the lodge with all—I said ALL—their things at nine tomorrow morning. The girls who are taking the Chicago train meet at the lodge at eleven."

"That's you, isn't it, Jenny?" Carol whispered.

"Oh yes," Miss Bugs said, "Jenny, you're to go to the Indian Village just as soon as you can this morning."

Up to this point the girls had been paying very little attention to Miss Bugs for they knew that these same instructions would be given over and over all through the day but with her last words they stopped whatever they were doing and looked at Jenny.

"She can't go to the Indian Village," Sarah objected. "Sunny Glade girls aren't allowed."

"If she goes they'll paint her face."

Someone giggled. "And it won't wash off and she'll have to get on the train tomorrow morning looking like an Indian."

"Oh no, she won't," Nadine said. "The girls at the Village won't paint Jenny's face. She's going by special invitation."

"How do you know so much about it, Nadine, we'd like to know?"

"It's a secret," Nadine said and winked at Jenny.

On her way to the Village Jenny decided to stop once more and try to see Miss Holly about the arrangements for her trip home. During the last two days she had stopped three times but each time Miss

Holly had been terribly busy and told her to wait until later.

Miss Holly looked just as busy today. Jenny stood outside her door and looked in. Miss Holly was packing her own things. "Oh, hello, Jenny," she said and looked a little dismayed.

"I guess this isn't such a good time either," Jenny apologized, "but I thought I ought to at least know if Uncle Fred is going to meet me in Chicago. Mother said you would tell me about everything. I'm afraid I'm being quite a bother about it though."

At once Miss Holly got up from the floor where she was sorting tennis shoes and came out on the porch beside Jenny. "You're certainly not a bother," she said. "No, it isn't that at all."

Well, Jenny thought, at last I'm going to find out about Uncle Fred.

Miss Holly looked thoughtful. Then she said brightly. "You know, Jenny, if I tell you all about the plans now you may very well forget them by tomorrow so why don't we wait until then?"

Miss Holly clearly didn't intend to discuss the matter any further so Jenny went on to the Indian Village. Although, as Nadine had said, she was going on a special invitation it still seemed queer to be entering the stockade that was the boundary line of the Village. Inside it was very exciting. There were real tepees of long poles and canvas, the sides rolled up so that she could see the log and rope beds. A black iron pot swung on a chain over a fire hole. There was more, much more and Jenny would have liked to look at every bit of it but Marilyn swooped down upon her and hurried her away to the place where Miss Eagle and the Village girls were gathered.

Jenny was given a feather headdress which was tied firmly on her head. "It looks wonderful," Marilyn said and Jenny hoped that it did.

They also provided Jenny with a beaded jacket, leggings and moccasins. These really were beautiful. For a final adornment there were wheels of feathers tied to her upper arms and on her ankles bands of bells so that every step she made was accompanied by a soft jingling.

Now the rehearsals began. In addition to the opening ceremonies of the Grand Council the Village girls were to perform the Cherokee Beaver dance. This was very complicated. The "beaver" was made of fur and attached to long ropes so that it could be dragged back and forth. The girls carried sticks and there was much waving of them and drumming and stomping.

"Girls," Miss Eagle said, almost in despair, "we'll have to do it again. You must all march in the same

148

direction and please try to not bang each other over the head."

One of the girls said, "Maybe the Fire Maker should have a practice, too."

"It isn't necessary," Marilyn assured them. "She's been practicing all summer. She can do it every time."

Jenny beamed with pleasure and shivered with fear. Just supposing tonight was the one time she couldn't do it at all!

6

The Grand Council

THE day fairly shot by. Jenny had her final swim and an early dinner and then it was time to report back to the Village to dress for the Grand Council. To her surprise Mr. Willie was outside the stockade, waiting for her. "Well, Fire Maker," he said, "this is your big night."

"Mr. Willie, I'm not sure I can do it. In fact I'm more sure every minute that I can't."

"Ridiculous," Mr. Willie said. "Of course you can. Just take it slow and easy. Remember, a good woodsman doesn't get excited and he does keep his wits about him. Now look, I brought you something." He took from his pocket a little sack and in it was the finest, dryest tinder Jenny had ever seen. "I made this special," Mr. Willie said. "It's guaranteed to fire up every time."

Jenny took the sack. "Thank you, Mr. Willie. Thank you for everything."

At the Village the girls were hurrying into their costumes. Already it was growing dusky for it was coming to the end of summer. After they were dressed they put paint on their arms and legs and faces. "I'll do Jenny," Marilyn said and she went to work with a great deal of enthusiasm and a great deal of paint. Jenny wondered what Uncle Fred was going to think when she got off the train the next day in Chicago.

"All right," Miss Eagle said, "it's time. Line up, everyone. Get the torches. Straighten your headdresses. Candy, get off that drum. Do you want to sit right through the middle of it? Then where would we be? Fire Maker, you stand right here behind the chief and the drummer."

The bearers with their unlighted torches moved forward and the procession started. The bells on Jenny's ankles chimed with each beat of the drum. She held the leather pouch tightly in her hand. The line approached the council ring and then it stopped. Jenny could see the white shirts of the girls glimmering in the fading light. Beyond them was a group of parents who had come to see the ceremony and who would take their daughters home with them after it was over. Tomorrow the camp would be very small.

Now the drumming commenced again and the procession moved forward. Slowly they circled the outside of the ring and then entered by the Council Rock. Silently, solemnly, the torch bearers took their positions on either side of the rock. The chief came in and the drummer and the dancers made a half circle behind. Now it was time for Jenny to step forward and make fire.

In the center of the great ring she knelt and emptied the little leather pouch. It was almost dark. She couldn't see a single face but it seemed to her that everyone in the world was out there watching, waiting.

Her hands were shaking as she made a little nest of the fine dry tinder and arranged the bit of cloth. As she lifted the flint in her hand she saw that drops of water had fallen to the ground on either side of the tinder. Rain! Oh, what should she do? She would never be able to make fire in the rain.

One more drop fell. Just one. She put her arm up to her forehead. The rain was coming from her. She was wet with perspiration. She wiped her face with the back of her hand and knelt above the little pile on the ground. "Calmly," Mr. Willie had said. "Carefully."

Jenny, the Fire Maker

She struck the flint across the steel. Sparks fell on the cloth, there was a fine wisp of smoke and then a very tiny flame. Jenny tended it until all the tinder caught fire and sent up flames.

There was a murmur from the girls around the council ring like the wind in the pines. Jenny stepped back. The bearers came forward and thrust their kerosene soaked torches into the fire and they flamed instantly. On the torches the fire was carried to the tower of logs and it was set ablaze.

Jenny went back and took her place just behind the circle of dancers. She still felt stiff and as if she

was moving in a dream. From behind her she heard Nadine. "I knew you could do it, Jenny," she whispered. "You were absolutely wonderful."

All at once Jenny relaxed and began to enjoy the beautiful ceremony. Miss Holly gave a farewell talk to the girls and they sang many of their songs. Then beaded leather honors were awarded. Jenny was called forward to receive two, one in swimming and one in nature lore. She was particularly surprised by the nature lore award. She hadn't supposed anyone would ever forget about the poison ivy disgrace. The Camp Craft honors were the last to be given out. As the other girls were called forward Jenny turned to Nadine. With her lips she formed the words, "Next year." Nadine smiled and nodded vigorously.

Now the Grand Council was over and the girls were making their way across the clearing and back to their cabins for the last time. Some of the girls had run to greet their parents and others were standing quietly listening to the last lonely notes of the bugle.

Jenny was standing by herself. Miss Holly came over. "You did so well, Jenny. And your surprise is here. Now don't get too excited—" Miss Holly was very excited.

Jenny looked over her shoulder and there, coming across the council ring, were her father and mother. Then Jenny got excited. The next ten minutes was a wild confusion of surprise and delight. Questions were asked that weren't answered and explanations made that weren't understood.

"I just can't believe it," Jenny said again. "I kept asking and asking Miss Holly about the plans for going home and she kept telling me to wait."

"I'm afraid we made things difficult for Miss Holly," her mother said. "But we weren't at all sure we could get here for Grand Council and then when we did and Miss Holly explained about your part in the ceremony we thought we'd better wait and not make you more keyed up than you already were."

"Anyway," Jenny said, "now I can stop wondering if Uncle Fred will be there to meet me on the way home."

"You aren't going home, Jenny," her father said. "That's the second part of the surprise. I'm going to be working on a book this winter and we're all going to live in Star Center in your mother's old home."

This called for another ten minutes of astonished questions and complicated explanations. "Are we going to Star Center now—tonight," Jenny asked her mother.

"No, in the morning. That is—your father is going back to New York to take care of some business and have our things shipped out but you and I are going to live for a time with Miss Holly."

"In the public library!"

"No, honey, I said with Miss Holly. I'm afraid all this excitement has been too much for you. And it is late. You'd better go up to the cabin with the girls now and I must talk to Miss Holly about our plans."

"First I'll have to go to Indian Village and return my costume."

Her father put his hand on her shoulder. "I'll go with you."

"Oh, you can't. If anybody goes into the Village without being asked, the girls will paint his face."

"Will they really?" Her father looked delighted. He began to move in the direction of the Village.

"You come with me, Peter," Mrs. Will said firmly and after a last hug for Jenny she started for Miss Holly's house.

But Mr. Will lingered. His hand still rested on Jenny's shoulder. "You've changed, Jenny. And how you have grown."

Dimly Jenny remembered his saying something of this sort to her the night before she left for Camp Tanda. She smiled at him. "And I've learned some things, too. I've learned not to boast. My goodness, I never go around now saying how good I am or how well I can do something."

Mr. Will began to laugh. "Oh, Jenny, what do

you think you're doing right now?"

Jenny clapped her hand over her mouth. Then she laughed, too. "Anyway," she said. "I'm trying."

"Good night, Fire Maker." Her father sounded proud.

She left him then and ran across the council ring toward the path that led to the Indian Village. At the far edge of the ring she stopped and looked back. It was empty now. Only the last little flames flickered in the ashes of what had been a blazing tower of logs.

The moonlight shone clearly on the white rocks that outlined the ring and silhouetted the encircling trees against the sky. Overhead the stars glittered. The summer had ended but she would be standing here again. She would be here in other summers and in the winter when white snow covered it all.

She drew a deep slow breath. My goodness, if she were the least bit happier she wouldn't be able to stand it. She'd simply explode. With the ankle bells jingling she sped up the hill to the Indian Village.